"I want to kiss you, but I'm not sure it's worth the risk." Hunter's voice was both smooth and rough, honey poured over gravel.

"Wh-what do you think will happen?" Millie was shocked at the sound of her own voice—whisper-soft, breathless with anticipatory excitement. Breathless with lust.

He nudged one side of her mouth with his lips, just a gentle bump of flesh on flesh, and yet it created a storm of sensation. Tingles, fizzes, darts of need that traveled straight to her core. His lemony aftershave intoxicated her senses. She felt tipsy—no, flat-out drunk and out of control. "Well, let's see... One, you might slap my face."

"I abhor violence of any type." Who was this person sitting in the car with him, almost kissing him? Acting coy and coquettish, as if she had written the handbook on flirting?

"Two, you might kiss me back."

Millie double blinked. "And th-that would be a problem?"

He smiled against the side of her mouth and a wave of incendiary heat coursed through her body.

"Yes. I might not want to stop kissing you."

Melanie Milburne

BREAKING THE PLAYBOY'S RULES

Recycling programs
for this product may
not exist in your area.

ISBN-13: 978-1-335-40332-2

Breaking the Playboy's Rules

Copyright © 2020 by Melanie Milburne

Harlequin Enterprises ULC
22 Adelaide St. West, 40th Floor
Toronto, Ontario M5H 4E3, Canada
www.Harlequin.com

Printed in U.S.A.

Melanie Milburne read her first Harlequin novel at the age of seventeen, in between studying for her final exams. After completing a master's degree in education, she decided to write a novel, and thus her career as a romance author was born. Melanie is an ambassador for the Australian Childhood Foundation and a keen dog lover and trainer. She enjoys long walks in the Tasmanian bush. In 2015 Melanie won the HOLT Medallion, a prestigious award honoring outstanding literary talent.

Books by Melanie Milburne

Harlequin Presents

Tycoon's Forbidden Cinderella
The Return of Her Billionaire Husband

Conveniently Wed!

Bound by a One-Night Vow

Once Upon a Temptation

His Innocent's Passionate Awakening

Secret Heirs of Billionaires

Cinderella's Scandalous Secret

The Scandal Before the Wedding

Claimed for the Billionaire's Convenience
The Venetian One-Night Baby

Wanted: A Billionaire

One Night on the Virgin's Terms

Visit the Author Profile page
at Harlequin.com for more titles.

To all the dedicated frontline medical workers soldiering on during the COVID-19 pandemic. You are all amazing to put your own lives on the line to help others. You sacrifice time with your own families, you work punishingly long hours and you support those who work alongside you. You are the true heroes of this era.

CHAPTER ONE

IT WAS THE first time in her life Millie had asked a man to meet her for a drink and now she was going to be late. Seriously, embarrassingly, late. But this was no ordinary date. This meeting with hotshot celebrity divorce lawyer Hunter Addison was not for herself but for her mother.

Her mother collected ex-husbands like some people collected coins. And, sadly, it was going to take an eye-watering amount of coins to get rid of husband number four—money that Millie could ill afford to lend her mum right now. Hunter Addison wasn't the cheapest divorce lawyer in London, but he was reputed to be the best.

And, for her mum, Millie wanted the best.

Millie walked as quickly as she could towards the wine bar where she'd asked Hunter to meet her after work. She hadn't spoken to him in person, only via text message. The thought of talking to him on the phone after their disastrous blind date two months ago was too confronting. So too was the prospect of meeting him again in person but this wasn't about her—it was about her mother's welfare. She could not bear to see her mother screwed over by yet another self-serving, narcissist ex.

Millie pushed open the front door of the wine bar and stepped inside, quickly scanning the room for any sign of Hunter. Couples and small groups were sitting at the various tables in the front section but there was no sign of a man sitting by himself. Of course, it would be incredibly rare for a man as good-looking, wealthy and sophisticated as Hunter ever to sit in a bar by himself. He had a reputation for being a fast-living playboy. Hardly a week went past when he wasn't snapped by the paparazzi with yet another gorgeous supermodel-type woman draped on his arm.

Interestingly, in the couple of months since their blind date, there had been nothing in the press about his sexual antics. Maybe Millie's immunity to his attractiveness that night had bruised his overblown ego. Not flipping likely. Men like Hunter Addison had industrial-strength egos. Trying to put a dent in his ego would be like trying to crack a brazil nut with a feather boa. Not going to work.

'You're late.' A deep and crisp male voice rich with censure spoke from behind her.

Millie spun round and, even though she was wearing vertiginous heels, she had to crane her neck up, up, up to meet Hunter Addison's whisky-brown eyes. It was hard not to feel a little flustered coming face-to-face with such arrant masculinity. Such heart-stopping male perfection. Broad-shouldered and tall, with a lean and athletic build, he exuded strength and potency. At a virile thirty-four, he was in the prime of his life and it showed.

And every female cell in her body sat up and took notice. 'Yes, I know. I'm sorry but—'

'Something wrong with your phone?' The smile that wasn't really a smile matched the cynical gleam in his eyes.

Millie mentally counted to ten, trying to control her desire to snap out a biting retort. What was it about this man that made her feel so prickly, on edge and so...so combative? Her experience around men was limited. She had only ever had one lover and, since her childhood sweetheart Julian had died three years ago after a long battle with brain cancer, she hadn't dated again.

Well, apart from the wretched blind date with Hunter, which had been an unmitigated disaster from start to finish. But then, she had *wanted* to sabotage it. She had done everything in her power to give him the cold shoulder and hot tongue routine. She was *not* going to be set up by friends to 'move on'. She was not going to be flirted with and charmed by a man who hadn't heard the word 'no' from a woman his entire life.

But now she needed Hunter's help and she had no choice but to swallow the choking lump of her pride. And boy, oh, boy did it taste sour.

Millie straightened her shoulders and forced herself to hold his gaze. 'There was, actually. I forgot to charge it overnight and it ran out of battery just after I left work. Then there was some sort of security incident involving the police on my way here and I had to take a six-block detour.'

In flipping sky-high heels and a tight-fitting pencil skirt, she wanted to add, but managed to restrain herself.

It was hard to tell if he believed her or not. His expression was now largely inscrutable and yet there was something about the way his eyes drifted to her mouth for the briefest of moments that made the backs of her knees tingle.

'Come this way. I have a table in the back where it's more private.' His tone had a commanding edge that made her want to insist on a table out front instead. He probably thought she regretted giving him the brush-off. He probably thought she wanted a rerun of their date.

But no. *No.*

This was not a cosy little *tête-à-tête*. This was not a date in any shape or form. This was a meeting to convince him to act for her mother. But she found herself—meekly, for her—following him to the table in the quieter back section of the wine bar.

Hunter waited until she was seated before he took the chair opposite. She was conscious of his long legs so close to hers under the small table and kept her knees tightly together and angled to the right to avoid any accidental touching. Millie was also conscious of the way her heart was beating—deep pounding beats that echoed in her ears as if her blood was sending out a sonar warning. *Danger.*

Hunter picked up the drinks menu and

handed it to her across the table. 'What would you like to drink?'

Millie took the menu and gave it a cursory glance before handing it back. 'Just mineral water, thank you.'

He made a soft sound of amusement and a sharper glint appeared in his eyes. 'Don't tell me you've gone teetotaller on me?'

Millie could feel a hot blush stealing over her cheeks. She had drunk three glasses of wine during their date, as well as a lethally strong cocktail, in an effort to get through the ordeal. The day of their disastrous date had been the anniversary of Julian's death, and each year she struggled to get through it— which was why her friends had organised the blind date with Hunter, hoping it would distract her and help her to move on. It had distracted her all right. Everything about Hunter Addison was distracting, back then and now. Especially now.

But it wasn't grief that had made that day so hard for her.

It was another G-word. Guilt.

Millie aimed her gaze to a point above his left shoulder rather than meet his probing gaze. 'No. I just don't feel like alcohol right now.'

Hunter signalled the waiter and ordered

Millie's mineral water and a gin and tonic for himself. Once the waiter had gone to fetch the drinks, Hunter leaned back in his chair with a casual ease she privately envied. He was dressed in a smart grey suit and snowy-white business shirt, the top button undone above his loosened, finely checked grey-and-white tie, giving him a chilled out, laid back air. He was devilishly handsome with short black hair, a straight nose and a sculptured mouth—the lower lip fuller than the top one. His late-in-the-day stubble shadowed his chiselled jaw and around his mouth, and he had a well-defined philtrum between his nose and top lip.

A sensual mouth...

Millie sat up straighter in her chair, shocked at her errant thought. She wasn't interested in his mouth. She was interested in his professional expertise. And the sooner she engaged it, the better. But right now it was almost impossible to get her brain into gear, to be logical and rational and stay on task. Every time he looked at her, flutters and tingles erupted in her flesh, as if he had closed the distance between them and touched her with one of his broad-span hands.

One thing she knew for sure—she must

not let him touch her. That would take her pretence of immunity way out of her skill set.

'So, here we are. Again.' Hunter's gaze went on a lazy perusal of her face, and something in her stomach turned over. And the way his voice leaned ever so slightly on the word 'again' made the roots of her hair tingle, as if tiny footsteps were tiptoeing over her scalp.

Millie licked her suddenly too-dry lips. She smoothed her skirt over her knees with her hands and tried to ignore the way her pulse was leaping. 'I feel I should apologise for how I behaved the last time we met.'

She chanced a glance at him and found him looking at her with studied concentration. Was that his lawyer face? The steady and watchful legal eagle quietly assessing his client. Reading between the lines of what his client said and what they did. But she wasn't his client. Although, she wasn't exactly a friend asking a favour either, was she? They had disliked each other on sight...or at least she had made up her mind she would dislike him.

She swallowed and continued. 'I wasn't in the best mood that night and I fear I might have taken it out on you.'

'You fear?' The edge of sarcasm in his voice was unmistakable.

Her chin came up and her gaze collided with his. 'Well, you were hardly Mr Dream Date yourself.'

Something shifted at the back of his gaze, as if he was mentally recalling that night and didn't like what he saw. A dull flush slashed high across his cheekbones and his lips twisted in a self-deprecating smile. 'Point taken. My charm button was on pause that night.'

As apologies went, it wasn't the most gracious, but then, she had been the one who had acted with the most appalling manners that night. He had been a little broody and distant, but she had been downright rude. She'd been annoyed at the matchmaking attempt of her friends, who had been at her for over a year to get out more. Beth and Dan were well-meaning, but they didn't know the real reason she found the prospect of dating again so difficult.

Julian had been sick for six years before he'd finally succumbed to his illness, diagnosed just before he'd turned eighteen. The treatment had been gruelling, the first operation changing his personality from loving

and kind to grumpy and short-tempered. But
Millie had hung in there, hoping month after
month, year after year, that things would get
better. They hadn't. The thought of breaking
up with him had not only crossed her mind,
it had taken up residence and patiently waited
for a good opportunity for her to raise it with
him. It had never come. Julian had always
been too sick, too depressed or in one of those
rare but wonderful phases when the cancer
seemed to be in remission.

How could she have destroyed him by saying she wanted out?

Millie was pulled out of her reverie when
the waiter appeared with their drinks and it
was a moment or two before she and Hunter
were alone again. Millie picked up her glass
for something to do with her hands. She took
a sip and covertly studied him. There should
be a law against men looking so hot without even trying. He exuded male potency and
she wondered what it would be like to be in
bed with him, those gym-toned legs entwined
with hers. Her mind ran wild with X-rated
images of his naked body in full arousal.

Sex with her late fiancé had been difficult
due to the ravages of his illness and his limited stamina. She had cared for Julian rather

than loved him and had allowed him to find quick pleasure in her body without insisting on her own. It had made her annoyed with herself rather than him, knowing he couldn't help being so ill. Since his death, she'd had fleeting thoughts about sex, but had never gone any further than occasional self-pleasure. Somehow, over the years with Julian and since his death, she had begun to associate all things sexual with disappointment, dissatisfaction and faint tinges of despair.

But now, sitting opposite Hunter, all she could think about was how it would feel to have his body thrusting within hers. She was pretty sure he would never leave a partner dissatisfied or disappointed. His sexual competence was an aura that surrounded him. Every time he locked gazes with her, she felt a jolt of electricity shoot to her core. She wriggled in her seat, her lower body restless, agitated, hungry, her cheeks feeling as hot as fire.

A slight frown settled between his ink-black eyebrows and, though he picked up his drink, he didn't take even a token sip. 'One wonders, if you had such a miserable time on our blind date, why on earth would you want to repeat it?' Hunter said, holding her gaze with his steely one.

Millie pressed her lips together. 'I don't. I wanted us to meet to discuss something… else.'

One of his eyebrows rose in a perfect arc. 'Go on.' His eyes never left hers—steady, strong, searching, sharply intelligent.

She ran the tip of her tongue over her parchment-dry lips, trying to ignore the way his gaze drifted downwards, as if he found the shape of her mouth fascinating. She drew in a breath and it shuddered through her chest like air in a damaged set of bellows. 'I want to engage your professional services.'

His eyes flicked to her left hand, where Julian's engagement ring still sat. Truth be told, Millie didn't especially like the ring, but she continued to wear it out of guilt. She knew Beth and Dan had told Hunter about Julian's death for he had mentioned it on their blind date. She had refused to discuss it with him and had abruptly changed the subject. 'You're not married. I'm a divorce lawyer. Not sure how I can help, unless there's something you're not telling me?'

There was a whole lot Millie wasn't telling him, or anyone else for that matter. She had a reputation among her friends as being a sniffer dog for other people's secrets. The thing was, she wasn't all that good at keeping them, unless they were her own secrets. She knew the tells of someone trying to keep something hidden, because for years *she* had being keeping things hidden. And doing a stellar job of it too.

She had not been in love with Julian. And, worse, she had actually felt something akin to relief when he had died three days before their wedding. She played the role of tragic heroine so well. Heart-sore and unable to love again after the tragic loss of her childhood sweetheart. Still wearing his modest little engagement ring after all this time. Still grieving her one and only love. Her soul mate.

But she was a big, fat fraud.

An imposter. Because, while she definitely grieved for the loss of a dear friend, Julian had not been the love of her life.

Millie leaned forward to pick up her mineral water, sat back again and looked at the ice cubes rattling against the glass for a moment. 'No, I'm not, but my mother is.' She brought her gaze to meet his and continued, 'Will you do it?'

Hunter held her gaze for so long without

speaking, she had to moisten her dry lips again. His eyes followed the movement and something behind her heart fluttered like a trapped insect. 'Why me?' His tone was curt, business-like, but his darkening brown eyes belonged in the bedroom. The flutter in her chest travelled to her stomach—soft little wings beating against the walls of her belly, sending an electric tingle down the backs of her legs.

Millie leaned forward in her chair to put her glass of mineral water back on the table. She was going for cool and calm and collected, but inside she was trembling with strange, unfamiliar sensations. Smouldering heat coursed through her body. Her heartbeat accelerated, her skin prickling and tingling behind the shield of her clothes. But pride wouldn't allow her to tell him the truth about her mother's situation.

That was another of her well-kept secrets. Diamond heiress Eleanora Donnelly-Clarke was practically penniless after multiple divorces. Millie's mother had been blessed with stunning beauty but had severe dyslexia. Each of her exes had taken advantage of her literacy and numeracy issues, and ex number four was about to do the same. If it wasn't for the trust fund Millie's grandfather had set up for Millie, both she and her mother would have gone under by now. But Millie had her own jewellery business to run and couldn't afford to carry her mother too much longer, especially in the event of another costly divorce—hence her appeal to Hunter.

Millie met Hunter's gaze. 'Because I've heard you're the best.'

One side of his mouth came up in a half-smile, as if he found her comment mildly amusing but of zero importance to his own estimation of his competence. One of his muscled arms was draped casually over the back of his chair, one ankle propped over his strong thigh, just above the knee. Unlike her, he had cool and calm and collected down to a science. 'And here I was thinking you were after a one-night stand with me.' His voice was deep and smoky, his smouldering eyes doing a slow appraisal of her face and figure.

Millie gave a stiff smile, showing no teeth. 'Sadly, no.'

A single eyebrow rose again, his eyes glinting. 'Sadly?'

Millie's heart rate shot up as if she were drinking rocket fuel instead of mineral water. She sat straighter in her chair. She had to do everything she could to keep her body from betraying her in the presence of his sensual charm. *Everything*, including keeping her wayward gaze away from his sinfully sculptured mouth. 'In spite of what Dan and Beth think, you're not my type.'

Hunter gave a slow smile that did serious damage to her determination to resist him. 'Nor you mine, but they seemed to think we'd be a match made in heaven. I wonder why?' His question was idly playful, rhetorical, even slightly mocking. Strike that—*definitely* mocking, drat the arrogant man.

'They're under the misguided impression that a fling with you will somehow help me move on from the loss of my fiancé,' Millie said in a tone so starchy and prim, she could have been lecturing young Victorian ladies on etiquette. 'But I'm afraid they have seriously over-estimated the extent of your charm.'

He gave a wry laugh, but then his expression gradually lost its teasing playfulness, his eyes becoming dark and more serious. 'I guess you'll move on when you're ready to.'

Millie lifted her chin and held his gaze. 'I'm not ready.' Would she ever be ready? When she'd been young and first fancied herself in love with Julian, getting married and setting up a home together was all she had wanted. But, when the hammer blow of his diagnosis had come, everything had changed. Her dream relationship had become a nightmare in reality.

Hunter's eyes moved between each of hers in a pulsing moment that ratcheted up her heart rate. Time stood still—so still she could hear the roaring echo of her heartbeat in her ears. He was a top-notch lawyer. He spent hours listening to clients, making sense of the things they told him, both true and false and all the shady spaces in between.

Could he see the truth behind her lie?

His eyes went to her mouth, lingering there for a heart-stopping moment, before coming back to her gaze. 'So, about your mother's divorce.' The subject change nudged her out of her thoughts. 'I should warn you, I don't come cheap.'

Millie tried to ignore the little niggle of panic about her bank balance. She was a moderately successful jewellery designer in an increasingly competitive market, but exorbitant legal fees were going to put a considerable dent in her savings. 'I can afford you.' She injected her tone with pride, her chin elevated.

Their gazes were locked in a power struggle for a beat or two but then he suddenly frowned. 'Why would you be the one paying your mother's legal fees?'

Millie lowered her shoulders in a despondent sigh. 'Because my mother's soon-to-be-ex spent a lot of her money in a get-rich-quick scheme that fell flat. Plus, she just found out he has a mistress on the side. Mum will pay me back once she gets back on her feet.' *If* she got back on her feet.

He studied her for another long moment that felt like an aeon. 'I'll do a deal with you. I'll give you a discount if you have dinner with me tomorrow night.'

Millie's mouth fell open. 'Dinner?'

One side of his mouth tilted upwards. 'You do eat occasionally, don't you?'

'Yes, but I thought, given what a disaster our last dinner was—'

'Maybe I want another chance to stun you with my charm.' A teasing glint appeared in his gaze.

'You said it yourself—you're not my type.'

'That doesn't mean we can't have a pleasant dinner together and clear the air after the last time.'

Millie wondered what motive was behind his invitation. Had her previous immunity to him presented him with a challenge he couldn't resist? She'd often wondered since that night, if they had met up on any other date other than the anniversary of Julian's passing, if she would have been quite so immune to him. In spite of her unfriendly behaviour that night, she *had* noticed his traffic-stopping good looks and superbly toned body. She had desperately tried not to notice but a woman would have to be brain dead and without a pulse not to be impressed by how gorgeous he was in the flesh.

In the flesh...

Her mind swam with images of him naked and her pulse shot up again. She schooled her features into a mask of cool indifference, as if his invitation was nothing to get excited about. No point feeding his morbidly obese ego. 'I'll have to check my diary.'

'So, check it.' He nodded his head towards her bag where her phone was housed, his tawny eyes containing a challenge. *Resist me if you can.*

Millie sent him a sideways look, picked up her bag and took out her phone. She gave her phone diary a cursory glance, knowing full well there was nothing scheduled for the following night.

Her mind was going up and down on a see-saw. Should she or shouldn't she meet him for dinner? He said he would give her a discount on her mother's legal fees. Was this his bargaining chip? The more time she spent with him, the more intrigued by him she was. She had never met a more confident and self-assured man. A man who set goals and went after them with a single-minded purpose. Exactly the sort of man she needed to help her mother get out of this latest financial hole. She put her phone back in her bag and clicked the fastening closed with a definitive snap. 'I'm free, as it turns out.'

'Good. Where do you live? I'll pick you up at seven.'

'Erm, that's not necessary. I can meet you, like I did the last time.'

An implacable light appeared in his unwavering gaze. 'Let's not do anything like we did it the last time. I'll pick you up and take you home.'

Millie decided against making an issue of it and gave him her address, then added, 'How soon can you meet with my mother? I know you're awfully busy and—'

'I'll clear a space first thing tomorrow morning. Eight a.m.'

Millie let out an audible breath of relief. 'That soon? I don't know how to thank you. But would you mind if I came with her for… support?'

'That's fine. Bring any necessary documentation with you—financial records of joint assets or debts, bank statements, tax returns, that sort of thing—plus a list of any questions you'd like to ask, and any relevant information about the other party. It will help speed up the process. How long has she been separated from her husband?'

'Only a couple of months.'

'How long have they been married?'

'Four years.' Millie waited a beat and added, 'She's been married three times before. They've all ended in divorce.'

Hunter didn't seem at all shocked, but then, she figured he dealt with this sort of thing day in and day out. People who had once passionately loved each other fighting it out as bitter enemies in court over the division of assets. He had taken her account of her mother's soon-to-be-ex's reprehensible behaviour with such implacable calm, as if he heard similar stories every day of the working week. She wondered if that was why he was such a freedom-loving playboy. Maybe he found the notion of long-term love nothing more than a Hollywood fantasy. Dealing with warring divorce parties would be enough to turn anyone into a romance cynic.

'Which of her ex-husbands was your father?' he asked.

'None of them.' Millie looked at the loosened knot of his tie rather than meet his gaze. 'He died a couple of months before I was born. I think it's why she's been so unlucky in love since. She tried to replace him but could never find someone good enough to fill his shoes. It's why she's always kept his name. It's the one thing she didn't get talked out of relinquishing by any of her subsequent husbands.'

Hunter uncrossed his ankle from where it was resting on his bent knee and leaned forward to pick up his drink. 'Life can be tough on some people.' He took a small sip of his drink and put it down again.

'Yes, it can…' Millie looked at her left hand where Julian's ring sat. Barely a day went past when she didn't think of him. Not because she still loved him, but because of how unfair life had been to his mother and him. Julian's life had stopped at his diagnosis—the life he had planned, that was. So too had his mother's, all her hopes and dreams for her only child shattered by that devastating diagnosis. The gruelling treatment and multiple surgeries had taken away Julian's potential, reducing him to a frailty that had angered and frustrated him in equal measure.

And Millie had been chained to his side through all of it, trapped by a sense of duty that, to this day, she couldn't free herself from feeling. Because she hadn't been honest about her feelings for Julian—platonic feelings, not romantic love.

Hunter's phone rang and he grimaced as he checked the screen. 'I'll have to get this. Sorry.' He rose from his chair and added, 'I'll be back in a minute.' And then he wove his way through the other tables, presumably to go outside to take the call in private.

Millie couldn't see the street from this section of the wine bar, so sat finishing her drink, wondering if she had done the right thing in asking him to help her mother. He was the best man for the job, but it would mean regular contact with him for her, as her mother's supporter. Some divorces were simple and clear cut, but none of her mother's divorces had been, and Millie had no expectation this one would be any different. Hunter was a disturbingly attractive man and she wasn't half as immune to him as she'd thought.

He's not your type. The words so helpfully supplied by her conscience were not as reassuring as they ought to be. Right now, she didn't care if he wasn't her type. She couldn't stop imagining what it would feel like to have that sensually sculptured mouth pressed to her own. She suppressed a little shudder and put down her empty glass.

Don't even think about it.

CHAPTER TWO

HUNTER'S HEART PRACTICALLY came to a stop every time he got a call from one of his sister's carers. He went outside to take the call away from the background noise of the wine bar. And away from anyone—most particularly Millie—listening in.

'Rupinder? Is everything okay?' He cupped one hand over his other ear to tone down the sounds of the busy street. His heart rate would never return to normal until he was assured everything was all right with his sister who had a rare genetic disorder. Emma required round-the-clock care and he had set her up in a nice townhouse close to her medical specialists, and organised and funded a team of full-time carers for her.

'Yes, everything's fine to do with Emma, but I just wanted to let you know I'm going to have to take a couple of weeks off due to my mother suddenly taking ill. She needs surgery, so hopefully I won't be too long off work, just till she gets back on her feet. Judy is going to fill in for me—is that okay with you?'

Hunter let out a sigh of relief that the emergency at hand had nothing to do with his sister this time. 'Of course. Take all the time you need.'

Too many phone calls over the years had brought news of Emma having yet another *grand mal* seizure or some sort of serious infection. Meningitis, bronchitis, pneumonia, sepsis…the list went on. The worry was a constant background humming in his brain. One of the worst seizures Emma had had was on the day of his blind date with Millie. He had come straight from visiting his sister in the hospital, where the specialists and medical students had gathered around her bedside, gravely talking amongst themselves about her rare condition and what remaining options there were. Hunter had never felt less like going on a date, and certainly not one organised by his friends.

He was the last person who needed help in the dating department. He had no trouble attracting beautiful women to his side—his biggest problem was getting rid of them. He wasn't interested in settling down with a nice girl someday. Who would take him on with Emma as part of the package deal? Hunter was her guardian and he held power of attorney now their mother was dead. Their father had washed his hands of them long ago and now had a new family. A *perfect* family.

Hunter had seen a photo of Millie Donnelly-Clarke at a society ball in the press a few months ago and had been intrigued by her. She had an untouchable air about her, regal and aristocratic, and he'd found himself agreeing to his friends' suggestion of a blind date with her.

But then Emma…

A lot of his life was dictated by his sister's problems. Ever since he'd been twelve years old when his parents had divorced, and Emma only seven, he'd had to step up and take on heavy responsibilities to do with the welfare, care and support of his sister—not to mention support his devastated mother, who hadn't coped with being deserted by Hunter's father. Abandoned and ripped off in the divorce by the man who had once claimed to love her, Hunter's mother had been left to raise two children, one of whom required constant care and numerous expensive therapies.

Hunter hadn't been in the best of moods when he'd met Millie for dinner and, given how prickly and unfriendly she had been, he hadn't bothered to dazzle her with his usual charm offensive.

But strangely, ever since, he hadn't been able to get her out of his mind.

Was it because she'd been the first woman to give him the brush-off since he'd been a gangly, awkward teenager? Because she was the only one that had got away and now he wanted another chance? He wasn't the sort of guy who couldn't handle a bit of rejection now and again. He wasn't exactly short of female attention. He only had to click his fingers and a beautiful woman would be his for the asking.

But something about Millie's immunity to him had got his attention. And kept it.

Hunter ended the call with his sister's carer, pocketed his phone and walked back into the wine bar. Millie was sitting bent over her phone and it gave him a chance to look at her before he joined her back at the table.

Her silvery blonde hair was long and lustrous, exactly like a skein of silk. Her figure was petite and slim and yet utterly feminine. The first thing he had noticed about her was her grey-blue eyes—they seemed to change colour with her mood. One minute they were a smoky grey, the other an ice-blue. Her complexion was the classic peaches and cream, with high aristocratic cheekbones, a ski-slope nose and an upturned mouth that had been the stuff of his night-time fantasises for the last couple of months, since their ill-fated blind date. He hadn't so much as laid a finger on her, not even to shake her hand in greeting, much less kiss her cheek. And yet, every male hormone in his body throbbed with the desire to do so.

When he'd received the text from her about meeting up for a drink, he had thought she'd changed her mind about him. It had put a spring in his step the whole way to the wine bar, wondering why she had changed her mind when he hadn't exactly been Prince Charming that night. But she hadn't contacted him for a rerun of their blind date. She wanted to engage his services as a lawyer for her mother, yet she had agreed to another shot at dinner. Tick. That was a win for him. He was looking forward to making up for the disaster of their last date. Never let it be said a woman walked away from a date with him without a smile on her face.

Hunter walked back to the table and she glanced up from her phone. One of her neat eyebrows rose and her smile had a cynical tilt. 'One of your many lovers checking if you're free this evening?'

Hunter rarely spoke to anyone about his sister's circumstances and was certainly not going to do so now.

'Not this time.' Hunter sat opposite Millie and picked up his drink. That was all the explanation he was prepared to give. He didn't need her sympathy. He didn't need endless questions about Emma's condition and treatment options. It was pointless talking about something that could never be fixed. Emma was a part of his life that was sectioned off, mostly out of the desire to protect her from intrusive attention, and not just from the press.

Emma had a loving and trusting nature, and quickly formed attachments to people, but when they left she was completely and utterly devastated, just as she had been when their father had abandoned them. In his early twenties Hunter had made the mistake of introducing her to a girlfriend who had made a big fuss of her, but then, when she'd broken up with him, Emma had been dropped too. Since then, he had never introduced his sister to any other lover. They were too temporary, and he didn't want them using Emma to 'impress' him.

'Would you like another?' He gestured to Millie's now-empty glass.

She shook her head, her lips twitching, as if she was trying not to smile. 'No, thank you. I like to keep a clear head when I'm talking to a lawyer.'

He laughed at her dry wit. 'Good for you.'

There was a strange little silence.

Hunter couldn't stop looking at the shape of her mouth—ripely curved, evenly full lips with tilted up corners, as if smiling was their preferred position. He wondered if her lips were as soft and pliable as they looked. Wondered why he was even tempted when she was exactly the sort of woman he usually avoided. She wasn't the type for a quick hook-up or short-term fling, even if her gaze kept drifting to his mouth as if she couldn't help it. She was still in love with her dead fiancé, for God's sake. Her fiancé's ring was still on her finger. But there was something about her that captivated him in a way he had never been captivated before.

'Why are you looking at me like that?' Her voice jolted him out of his study of her face.

He gave a slow blink and brought his gaze back to meet hers. 'You know exactly why I'm looking at you like that. You've been looking at me exactly the same way.'

Two small circles of colour bloomed in her cheeks. 'Don't be ridiculous.'

Hunter gave another soft laugh and rose to his feet. 'I'll see you tomorrow in my office at eight a.m.' He handed her a business card with his contact details on it. 'This is just the initial consultation to get the ball rolling. I usually meet with my clients several times, depending on how things go, and how cooperative the other party.'

'Thank you.' Her index and middle fingers ever so lightly brushed against his palm as she took the business card from him, and lust slammed him in the groin. As first touches went, it was tiny, and yet it packed a knockout punch to his senses. His body tingled from head to foot and he could only imagine what would happen if he kissed her. That she had felt something too was obvious in the way she'd pulled her hand away, as if it had received an electric shock.

She slipped the card into her bag and rose

from her chair. Her teeth sank into her lower lip and she added, 'Erm, would you mind if you didn't mention anything about us having dinner tomorrow evening, when my mother comes to your office in the morning?'

Hunter wondered why the need for secrecy. Most women he took out to dinner couldn't wait to broadcast who they were seeing to all and sundry. It was a refreshing change, and an intriguing one that his 'date' with Millie be considered something to be kept private. 'No problem. It can be our little secret.'

Millie stood with her mother outside Hunter's office building the following morning with her heart doing funny little trots, hops and skips. 'Right. Here we go.'

'Are you sure he's the right person to act for me?' her mother asked, casting her a worried glance. 'I've heard he's terribly expensive.'

Millie linked her arm through her mother's. 'Don't worry about the expense. Think of the outcome. He's the one to get the job done. "Get him and get justice" is his tagline.'

Eleanora chewed her lip. 'You haven't told him about my—?'

'No, Mum. I haven't.' Millie was well used to covering up her mother's literacy issues.

She had been reading and interpreting letters and documents for her mum since childhood. Her mother could sign her name and read basic sentences, but legal documents could be hard for anyone, let alone someone with severe dyslexia. Millie knew her mother felt great shame about her problem, but every time Eleanora had taken a remedial class she had given up after only one or two sessions. She relied on her current partners or Millie to do things for her. At times, she even relied on her household staff—some of whom had also taken advantage of her.

They took the lift to the top floor of the building where Hunter's suite of offices was housed. The shiny brass plaque read: *Addison and Associates, Legal Services*, and the swish reception looked like the foyer of a top-notch hotel. Plush ankle-deep carpet, a finely crafted timber credenza and priceless works of art on the walls spoke of a legal eagle who was at the top of his game. The beautifully dressed, coiffed and made-up young female receptionist behind the polished credenza gave a welcoming smile that was blindingly white. 'Good morning.'

'Good morning,' Millie said, with an answering smile. 'We're here to see Hunter Addison. Millie and Eleanora Donnelly-Clarke.'

'I'll tell him you're here.' The receptionist leaned towards an intercom on her desk, which was connected to her headset and microphone, and informed Hunter of their arrival. Millie didn't hear his reply, but the receptionist pressed the 'off' switch and pushed back her chair. 'I'll take you to his office right now. Come this way.'

Millie and her mother followed the receptionist down a wide corridor with more beautiful works of art, a mixture of modern and classical, that somehow didn't clash at all but worked in perfect harmony. The receptionist opened the corner-office door—of course he had the corner office—and indicated for Millie and her mother to go in.

Millie stepped over the threshold and her eyes went straight to Hunter seated behind his polished mahogany and leather-topped desk. Behind him was the most spectacular view over London, and if he hadn't been so heart-stoppingly handsome she would have been tempted to stare at the view rather than at him. But no view could ever rival his superb male form. He was wearing a crisp white business shirt with a blue tie with silver stripes, the charcoal-grey jacket of his suit hanging off the back of his chair. He rose from his chair with a welcoming smile and her breath caught somewhere between her lungs and her throat.

'Good morning.' He came from behind the desk and offered his hand to Eleanora first. 'Eleanora, nice to meet you.'

'And you too,' Eleanora said, blinking rapidly and blushing as if she had just been introduced to a rock star.

Hunter then offered Millie his hand. She disguised a quick swallow and slipped her hand into his. The gentle but firm pressure of his long, strong, tanned fingers closing around hers sent a shock wave throughout her entire body. Flickers, darts and tingles passed from his hand to hers in a current of electricity that made the fine hairs at the back of her neck stand up. His fingers were warm and dry, and she couldn't stop thinking of how they would feel gliding over other parts of her body…her breasts, her thighs… His eyes meshed with hers and her heart did a somersault in her chest, the sensual heat of his palm and fingers travelling through her body to stir warm liquid longing in the secret heart of her female flesh.

'I hope our eight a.m. meeting wasn't too early for you to get out of bed?'

His deep voice and the smouldering glint in his whisky-brown eyes sent another wave of heat through her. She was aware of her body's quiet but chaotic response to him. The fluttering of her pulse, the molten heat of arousal between her legs, the near-desperate urge of her body to get closer to him. It was like the powerful pull of a magnetic force drawing her to him, one she had to do something—anything—to counteract.

Millie slipped her hand out of his, but it continued to tingle, as if his touch had permanently disrupted the network of her nerves, like a powerful lightning strike on a computer. 'No, not at all. I'm an early riser.'

The glint in his gaze brightened. 'So am I.'

Millie could only imagine what part of himself to which he was referring as an early riser. Her mind was suddenly filled with images of him in a tangle of sheets, his gloriously naked body in full arousal. She could feel her cheeks glowing and her mouth went completely dry. She took a step backward to put more distance between them, and somehow almost lost her footing, but his hand shot out just in time and steadied her.

'Careful.' His fingers were a steel bracelet on her wrist and a shiver travelled the length of her spine as she thought about where else those fingers could touch her. Where else she *wanted* them to touch her. She was shocked at her body's betrayal. It had been years since she had even thought of her sexual needs and urges. Her sensuality had been put in a coma by her experience of taking care of Julian's needs. But now, with just a touch of Hunter Addison's hand, a wave of sexual awareness swept through her body, awakening her sleeping senses, stirring them into a feeding frenzy.

The hunger in her body was out of control. Could he sense it? Could he see the impact his touch had on her? She prided herself on being good at hiding what she was really feeling but she wondered if Hunter would all too easily see through her mask of indifference to the burning, yearning hunger buried deep inside her.

'Thank you.' Millie gave him what she hoped was an impersonal smile and his hand fell away from her wrist.

'Take a seat and let's get started,' Hunter said.

'Here's the paperwork you asked for,' Eleanora said, pushing a folder of documents across his desk. Millie could see her mother's nervousness but hoped Hunter would assume it was only because of the stress of going through yet another divorce. Millie had attended many meetings with her mother in the past—lawyers, accountants, doctors and even her own parent-teacher interviews as a child and teenager—all in an attempt to protect her mother from the shame of exposure of her severe learning disability.

'Great, thanks,' Hunter said. 'The less research I have to do on your behalf, the less money you have to pay me. But I'll try and keep expenses down as much as possible.' He picked up a pair of rectangular horn-rimmed glasses from his desk and put them on, pushing them further up the bridge of his nose with his index finger. Millie couldn't have taken her eyes off him even if she'd tried. The glasses only made him look more attractive. Dangerously attractive.

After a couple of minutes, Hunter glanced up from the documents to address Eleanora. 'The property in Surrey—that was in your name originally?'

Millie jumped in to help her mother out. 'It was left to Mum by her father-in-law, my paternal grandfather, but it was put in both Mum's and Derek's names soon after their marriage.'

Hunter gave a slow nod, his expression mostly unreadable, but Millie could almost see the working of his clever brain behind the screen of his brown eyes. Processing, calculating, assessing, analysing. 'And these shares that were sold in January…' he again aimed his comment directly at Eleanora '…which account did the money go into after the sale? Or was it used to pay off debt?'

Eleanora looked at him blankly for a moment but, when Millie opened her mouth to speak on her behalf, Hunter put his hand up in a silencing gesture and she clamped her lips together. 'Eleanora?' he prompted.

Eleanora flicked a worried *Help me* glance at Millie before turning back to face him. 'I—I don't really know. I always let my husband see to that side of things. He's got more of a head for business than I do.'

He quietly assessed Eleanora for a nanosecond before responding, 'That's okay. Lots of married couples manage things that way.'

He leafed through a few more of the documents and Millie held her breath until she thought her lungs would explode. She hadn't been happy about Riversdale being changed into Derek's name, but it had happened before she could do anything to stop it. Riversdale was where her father had grown up and it pained her to think it might have to be sold to cover legal costs. It was her only link to the father she had lost before she'd been born.

But it might not just be Riversdale on the line. She'd barely had time to cast her own eyes over the papers before the appointment with Hunter but she'd seen enough discrepancies to raise her alarm. Large sums of money had been taken out of her mother's accounts. Why hadn't she stepped in earlier to protect her mother? Why had she let it come to this? It was financial abuse and it had happened—*again*—on Millie's watch.

After another few minutes that felt like an era, Hunter took off his glasses and placed them on top of the sheaf of documents on his desk, a small frown pulling at his brow. 'Okay, here's what I think we need to do. I have a friend who is a forensic accountant—one of the best, if not the best. Matteo Vitale. He's based in Italy, but he travels back and forth to London for work. If you're agreeable, I'll get him to run his eyes over your accounts and track all the activity during your marriage. Hopefully, it won't take too long, then we'll be in a better position to choose our approach going forward.'

'Thank you so much,' Eleanora said, looking vastly relieved.

Millie echoed her mother's thanks and added, 'It's very good of you to see us at such short notice.'

Hunter's gaze met hers and something warm and treacly slithered down her spine. 'The pleasure has been all mine.'

Millie rose from her chair with more breathless haste than grace and dragged her mother up with her. 'We should let you get on with your busy day. Come on, Mum.'

Hunter rose from behind his desk and came round to shake her mother's hand. 'Eleanora, would you be so kind as to give me a couple of minutes alone with Millie? We have some other business to discuss. My receptionist will get you a coffee or tea.'

'Of course,' Eleanora said, beaming and clasping his hand with both of hers, as if she was going to crush it with gratitude. 'I don't mind at all. Take all the time you need.' She finally released his hand, turned and left his office before Millie could do or say anything to stop her.

Hunter turned his gaze back to Millie. Dark, penetrating, intuitive. 'How well do you know your mother's husband?'

'Well enough to know I don't like him.'

'Did you ever like him?'

'Not really. He was charming at first, but I didn't like the way he spoke to mum once he got a ring on her finger. Or how he convinced her to put his name on the Riversdale deed without telling me.'

Hunter let out a short, harsh breath that sounded as if it might be code for *What a low-life bastard and I can't wait to nail him for it*. 'I'll try to sort this out for her as quickly and efficiently as possible.'

'Thank you.' Millie's heart began to thump as if she'd run up the fifty floors instead of using the lift. How would she pay for a long-drawn-out battle in court for her mother? She couldn't expect Hunter to reduce his fees. He hadn't become one of the richest lawyers in London by doing pro bono work, especially for someone like her—a woman who had been insultingly rude the first time they'd met. 'I really don't want to take up any more of your time, so…' She began to turn away but for the third time in the space of minutes one of his hands came down on her wrist.

'Wait. Stop trying to run away.'

She stared at his tanned fingers against the cream of her silk sleeve and something in her stomach swooped. She couldn't stop thinking of those long, tanned fingers on other parts of her body. Parts of her body that were already tingling as the warmth from his touch seeped into her skin irrespective of the silk barrier of her top. She slowly brought her gaze back up to his. 'Please, let me go.' Her voice came out as a hoarse whisper, but she was worried her eyes were saying the opposite. *Please, hold me.*

He drew in a breath and released her wrist, and then expelled his breath on a heavy sigh. 'I probably don't need to tell you I'm worried about your mother's situation. It looks to me like her current partner is siphoning off funds into hidden accounts but that's only a hunch at this stage. But, let me assure you, I will get to the bottom of it.'

'Thank you.'

He gave a brief smile that melted her resolve to keep her distance like a blowtorch on butter. She could actually feel her stiff and guarded posture relaxing and wondered how on earth she was going to resist him if he didn't stop being so much of a helpful hero to the rescue.

'Try not to worry too much.' His tone was gently reassuring and melted another layer of her emotional armour.

'Lately, all I seem to do is worry about my mother. For years, actually,' Millie found herself confessing. 'She has appalling taste in men. She falls for good looks instead of good character. And they fall for her because she's beautiful and compliant, like most men seem to want their women to be.'

'Not all men,' Hunter said, holding her gaze with gleaming intensity. 'Personally, I like a bit of spirit and push-back.'

Millie swallowed and glanced at his mouth, her stomach bottoming out. She moistened her lips and hitched in a ragged breath. Was he flirting with her? Yes, he was, and, even more worrying, she was enjoying it. Way too much. 'Erm, what other business did you want to discuss with me?'

He stepped close enough to touch her. Close enough to set her heart rate stampeding again. Close enough for her to see the tiny dark-chocolate flecks in his mid-brown eyes and the impossibly thick and long lashes that fringed them. Close enough for her to smell the light citrusy tang of his aftershave, redolent of sun-warmed lemons with a woodsy understory. He had shaved that morning, but tiny pinpricks of regrowth were already evident, suggesting he hadn't been standing back and holding the door for everyone else when the testosterone had been handed out.

Millie hadn't been this close to such a virile man in years. Possibly ever. His sensual energy brushed against her in soundless waves, sending shivers, darts and flickers of awareness across her skin.

Hunter picked up a section of her long silver-blonde hair and lightly trailed it across his fingers like someone inspecting a skein of priceless silk. His expression was inscrutable, all except for the dark intensity of his eyes. 'Why are you frightened of me?' His voice was low and deep with an edge of huskiness that made her skin lift in a delicate shiver.

'I—I'm not.' It would have sounded a whole lot more convincing if her voice hadn't come out as a scratchy whisper. And if her heart wasn't beating as if it was going to work its way out of her chest and her legs threatening to fold underneath her.

'Liar.' He gave a lazy smile and tucked her hair behind her ear, then lowered his hand back by his side. But he stayed close to her, so close all she had to do was move forward half a step and her breasts would be in contact with his chest and her pelvis in contact with his. Her breasts began to tingle behind the lace cage of her bra, hot little tingles that made her aware of her female form in a way she had never been before. A pulse beat between her legs—a delicate contraction of intimate muscles waking from a long hibernation.

Millie licked her carpet-dry lips. 'You're too close to me. I can barely breathe.'

'So, step back. I'm not stopping you.'

She lifted her chin, her eyes warring with his in a battle of wills. He liked a bit of push-back, did he? She could give as good as she got. 'Why don't *you* step back?'

His eyes smouldered. 'I like seeing the effect I have on you.'

Millie steeled her spine, iced her gaze and stood her ground. 'You have zero effect on me.'

The air beat with tension—sexual tension that disturbed the atmosphere like a galaxy of hyperactive dust motes.

His gaze snared hers and there was nothing she could do to break the deadlock. 'I look forward to making you eat those words one day in the not-too-distant future.' The deep rumble of his tone sent a runaway firework fizzing and whizzing down every knob of her spine.

Millie gave a tight-lipped smile when what she really wanted to do was slap his face for his arrogance. 'Don't hold your breath.'

He gave a soft chuckle of laughter and stepped away from her and strode idly over to the door of his office, effectively bringing their private meeting to a close. 'I'll see you tonight. I'll pick you up at seven.'

Millie wanted to tell him where to stick his dinner date, but she needed him on side for the best result for her mother's divorce. She needed him as an ally, not an enemy.

And most of all she needed her head examined for looking forward to seeing him again.

Hunter closed the door once Millie left and walked back to his desk with a smile. Hot damn, but he was excited about their dinner tonight. Excited in a way he hadn't been in years. He had never had to talk someone into having dinner with him before. Usually, he asked, and they said yes. But he'd had to *convince* Millie.

Who knew how attractive a woman playing hard to get could be? He liked her spirit, the light of stubbornness in her grey-blue eyes. His office still carried a trace of her perfume, teasing his nostrils with the beguiling scent of sweet peas and sultry summer nights.

It had been all he could do to keep his hands off her. Drawn to her with such fierce attraction, he had been tempted to kiss her to see what happened. But he wasn't the type of man to force himself on a woman. He would only kiss her when he was certain it was what she wanted—or, even better, if she made the first move. Unless he had read her completely wrong, she was fighting her attraction to him. Stubbornly resisting the sexual energy that erupted between them.

Was it because of her late fiancé? Beth and Dan had told him it had been three years since Millie's fiancé's death. At twenty-six, she was way too young to give up on dating. Not that he would be offering her anything but a temporary fling. He wasn't interested in tying himself down to one person. He wasn't interested in falling in love, the way his mother had fallen in love with his father and then had that love rejected, destroyed, poisoned by a brutally cold abandonment.

Not that Hunter could ever see himself sink to the lows of his father. It took a special type of lowlife to walk out on a child with a disability and never see her again. A child who loved her father devotedly and who, to this day, still couldn't understand what she had done wrong for him to abandon her.

Hunter sat back at his desk and looked back over the documents Millie's mother had provided. Alarm bells had rung as soon as Eleanora had walked into his office. He could definitely see where Millie got her stunning looks from but, unlike Millie, Eleanora had a submissive and compliant nature, like so many of his clients who got done over in a divorce—his own mother being a case in point. Financial abuse was a scourge—all forms of domestic abuse were—but he was not going to rest until he brought to light the dark dealings of yet another partner who thought they could get away with it.

But he had a gut feeling there was more to Eleanora's situation than either she or Millie were letting on. He had been a lawyer long enough to be able to read between the lines of what people said or didn't say, the inner emotions they desperately tried to conceal. It was his job to make sense of the grey areas, the black spots, the shadows, the secrets and lies.

He picked up the gold pen his sister Emma had bought for him for his last birthday, when she'd been out with one of her carers, and flicked it back and forth between his fingers, his mind replaying every moment of his meeting with Millie and her mother. Millie had answered for her mother as though she'd been the adult and Eleanora the child. He did it himself with his sister, because Emma had limited understanding of how the world worked and in many ways would always remain a child in an adult's body. He clicked the pen on and off, his mind still ticking over like the cogs of a machine. He dropped the pen back on his desk and pushed a hand through his hair.

This was exactly the sort of case he liked working on—bringing justice to those who needed it most. But, in order to do his job to the best of his ability, he needed to know the truth about his clients. The whole truth and nothing but the truth. And it was his job, his responsibility, to get it out of them, no matter what.

CHAPTER THREE

MILLIE RUSHED HOME from work later that day to get ready for her dinner with Hunter. Ivy Kennedy—one of her two flatmates—was in the process of moving out in preparation for her wedding in a few weeks' time. She looked up from where she was kneeling on the floor, packing a box of her kitchen utensils, when Millie came in.

'How did your meeting with Hunter Addison go? Is he going to act for your mum?'

Millie slipped her tote bag off her shoulder and hung it over the back of one of the kitchen chairs. 'Yep. It went well. He's organising a forensic accountant to go over all of mum's accounts to see if there are any irregularities. She was so relieved, I thought she was going to hug him.'

Ivy got up from the floor and pushed her auburn hair out of her face. 'I'm so glad you were able to put your prejudices aside and contact him again.' She smiled and added playfully, 'You obviously didn't completely burn your boats with him. He wouldn't have offered to do it if he couldn't stand a bar of you. Ha-ha, no pun intended.'

Millie was conscious of her cheeks heating and turned away on the pretence of taking her phone out of her tote bag. 'It's just another case for him. Nothing else.'

Ivy frowned and came a little closer. 'Is something wrong? You seem a little distracted. I thought you said the meeting went well?'

'It did, but this fourth divorce has made me realise how truly vulnerable Mum is, and how I can't really protect her the way I want to. I feel like I've let her down yet again. But I have my own business to run and I don't want to fail at it. I don't know how I can continue to be a good daughter and a good business-woman at the same time.'

'Why do you always feel so responsible for your mum?' Ivy asked. 'She's an adult—and, yes, like my mum she's been terribly unlucky in her relationships—but that's not your fault. Anyway, you have your own life to live. You gave so much of it up for Jules, helping him through his treatment and so on. You can't keep putting your own needs on hold indefinitely.'

Millie wished she could share the burden of her mother's problems but for years she had kept silent out of respect for her mother's feelings. She trusted her friends, Ivy and Zoey, would be nothing but supportive and understanding if she told them, but she had kept it a secret for so long, she didn't know how to put it into words. Would they feel hurt she hadn't told them earlier? And, if she revealed *that* secret, how soon before she revealed her own more shameful one?

She hadn't been, and wasn't still, in love with Julian.

Millie looked at her friend and grimaced ruefully. 'I only hope she doesn't fall for another guy who only wants her for her beauty and her money, or at least what's left of her money.'

Ivy gave her a warm hug. 'You're a wonderful daughter and a wonderful support to everyone who knows and loves you.' She leaned back, smiled and added, 'And you'll make a wonderful bridesmaid. Will you do it? I want you and Zoey to be my bridesmaids.

Zoey has already said yes, and it would be just divine if you did too.'

Millie smiled back, thrilled to be asked. 'Oh, wow, yes, of course! I've never been a bridesmaid before.'

Ivy glanced at the ring on Millie's left hand, a small frown of concern etched on her features. 'You won't find it…triggering, given you didn't get to have your own wedding?'

Millie shook her head, painting a smile on her mouth. 'I'll be fine. I'm just so happy you and Louis found each other.'

'I hope you find someone as special as Louis,' Ivy said, glowing with happiness at her upcoming wedding to the man of her dreams. 'Hey, maybe you and Hunter Addison will hit it off. Opposites attract and all that!'

'Don't be ridiculous.' Millie screwed up her nose, as if being with Hunter was the worst thing she could ever imagine.

Ivy's eyes began to twinkle. 'Never say never, my girl. Look what happened to me.'

Millie gave her a quelling look. 'You actually liked Louis and were already friends with him before you fell in love with each other. Hunter Addison and I can't spend an evening together without getting into a fight. Which is a problem because, in about an hour, I'm going to be spending the evening with him.'

Ivy gasped. 'On another date, you mean? Seriously?'

Millie shifted her lips from side to side. 'It's just dinner. I think he's only asked me because he's arrogant enough to assume I won't give him the brush-off a second time.'

'And will you?' Ivy asked, eyebrows raised. 'Give him the brush-off?'

Millie affected a laugh. 'But of course. He's not my type.'

And he damn well better stay that way, otherwise she was going to be in seriously big trouble.

Hunter arrived right on the dot of seven and Millie answered the door to his brisk knock with a cool smile on her face. 'Hi.' She tried not to notice how gorgeous he looked in a butter-soft black leather jacket and dark trousers teamed with a white open-necked shirt. Tried but failed. Her pulse kicked up its pace and her senses swooned at the crisp citrus notes of his aftershave and the dark glitter in his gaze.

'Hello there.' His deep voice did strange things to her heart rate, so too did the way his eyes ran over her baby-blue knee-length dress and cream pashmina wrap. 'You look very beautiful. That colour brings out the blue in your eyes.'

'Thank you.' A flutter of nerves erupted in her belly and she took a steadying breath, releasing it in a stuttered stream.

Hunter quirked a dark brow at her. 'Nervous?'

Millie lifted her chin and speared his gaze. 'Should I be?'

He lifted a hand to her face and trailed his fingertip from the top of her cheekbone to the base of her chin, his touch so light it barely grazed her, and yet her skin tingled as if touched by fire. 'Not with me.' His voice had gone down another semitone—deep, gravelly, sensual.

Millie rolled her lips together and looked at the open neck of his shirt where she could see a sprinkling of his dark chest hair—a heady reminder of the male hormones powering through his body. 'It's been a while since I went out to dinner with a guy.' She gave him a rueful smile and added, 'Well, apart from with you that last time, I mean.'

He gave a lopsided smile in return. 'Let's not talk about that night, hmm?' He placed his hand on her elbow. 'Shall we go? My car is just down the street a bit.'

Millie was conscious of the gentle warmth of his hand at her elbow, guiding her to where his car was parked a few doors down from her flat. His touch sent little aftershocks through her body. At six foot four, he towered over her, even though she was wearing heels. She had rarely worn heels going out with Julian, as he had only been a couple of inches taller, and somehow she had got into the habit of wearing flats so as not to make him feel inadequate.

Hunter helped her into the car, and she thought of all the times the role had been reversed in her relationship with Julian. Not that Julian had been able to help it, of course, but Millie had been the one to help *him* into the car, pulling down his seatbelt and making sure he was comfortable at all times and in all places. She had morphed into his carer rather than his partner and she'd had to suppress her resentment at how the tables had turned. Julian hadn't been to blame—it was his illness. If anyone had been to blame, it was her for not being honest with him from the get-go.

They spoke about inconsequential things

on the way to the restaurant—the weather, the news, the state of the economy—and all the while Millie was aware of him sitting close enough for her to reach out and touch him. He drove with competence and care, no risks or tricky manoeuvres, but with patience and consideration for the other road users. Her gaze kept going to his left thigh, and she wondered what it would feel like to run her hand up and down those powerful muscles. To feel them bunch under the gentle pressure of her fingers, to explore his body in intimate detail.

Millie turned her gaze to the front of the car and sat up straighter in her seat, annoyed with the way her mind kept wandering into such dangerous territory. Why was she so darn attracted to him? She hadn't thought herself the shallow looks-are-everything type. She hadn't thought herself all that impressed by a man's wealth or status. She hadn't thought she could ever be tempted to sleep with a man again.

That part of her life was over...wasn't it?

A few minutes later, Hunter led her into a fine-dining restaurant in Mayfair. They were taken to their table by a courteous waiter who addressed Hunter by name. Within a short time, they were seated with drinks in front of them. Hunter had declined alcohol, and she was secretly impressed he had made that choice, given he was driving. She had opted for mineral water again, keen to keep her head in his disturbingly attractive company.

Hunter raised his glass of Indian tonic water, his mouth tilted in a crooked smile. 'So, here's to second chances.'

With just a moment's hesitation, Millie lifted her glass to his. 'To second chances.'

The chink of their glasses sounded loud in the silence, their eyes locking over the table. A second chance at what—seduction? A one-night stand? A fling? The possibilities seemed to hover in the space between them. Sensual possibilities she hadn't allowed herself to think about until now. What would it be like sleeping with a man like Hunter? A man who had sexual experience on a scale she hadn't encountered before. She and Julian had been each other's one and only lover. Childhood sweethearts who had drifted into an intimate relationship that hadn't had a chance to grow and mature as it should, due to the impact of his illness. Over time, Julian hadn't had stamina or patience for her needs, and she had settled for a peaceful rather than passionate life.

But now her frozen passions were thawing, creating molten heat in her body she could no longer ignore, especially in the presence of Hunter. He triggered a fiery response in her with every glance, every touch. Who knew what would happen if he kissed her?

Could she risk such a conflagration of the senses?

Millie finally managed to drag her eyes away from his mesmerising gaze and took a tentative sip of her mineral water, wishing now she had asked for something stronger.

'Tell me about your fiancé.' The request was bluntly delivered, a command rather than a question, and it jolted her as if he had slammed his hand down on the table.

She drew in a quick breath and put her glass down, not quite meeting Hunter's gaze. 'I'd rather not, if you don't mind.' She wasn't going to spill all to him of all people. She hadn't even told her best friends the truth about her relationship with her late fiancé. Even her own mother knew nothing of Millie's tortured emotions over Julian.

'You find it painful?' His tone was disarmingly gentle.

Yes, but not for the reasons you think.

How could she tell him the truth about her

relationship with Julian? How could she tell anyone? Millie chanced a glance at him to find his expression etched in lines of concern. 'Have you ever lost someone you loved?' she asked.

A shadow passed through his whisky-brown gaze. 'Yes. My mother. She died ten years ago. Cancer. We were close.' His tone was matter-of-fact, delivering a set of details dispassionately, and yet his eyes told another story. A story of loss and sadness that hadn't yet been resolved.

'I'm so sorry,' Millie said. 'Do you still have your father?'

He gave a snort that sounded more like a suppressed cynical laugh. 'The truth is, I never *had* my father. I just thought I did.' His hand curled into a fist where it was resting on the table. 'He left us when I was twelve. Completely walked out of our lives and didn't once look back.' His fingers uncurled and he picked up his glass again. 'He has a new family now. A wife, two perfect kids.' He used the same dispassionate tone but underneath she could hear the steely thread of anger.

Millie could see the same anger written on his features. It was in every tense muscle of his face. She could only imagine how devastated he must have felt as a young boy on the threshold of manhood to be left by his father in such a brutally callous way. No contact over the tough years of adolescence, no mentoring through young adulthood, no relationship at all.

How had Hunter coped with such heartless rejection? It gave her an inkling of why he was such a driven and goal-oriented man. Didn't they say that rejection from a parent in childhood could make someone strive to over-achieve all their life in an effort to make up for the abandonment? But it was a never-ending quest—it could not be resolved unless harmony was restored with the absent parent and yet in Hunter's case it sounded as if the chance of that sort of reunion was next to impossible. 'That must have been so terribly hurtful for you, especially at that age. Actually, at any age.'

'More so for my mother and sister.'

'You have a sister?'

Something flickered over his features and a shutter came down in his gaze. 'Emma is five years younger. Our father's desertion hit her much harder than me. She worshipped the ground he walked on.' The hard and bitter note in his voice was gone, and in its place was a sad resignation about things that had happened and couldn't be changed.

Millie found herself leaning closer to him, desperate to offer some sort of comfort, some measure of understanding. 'I'm so sorry to hear that. Little girls often idealise their fathers. He's usually the first man they fall in love with. You must be very angry with him even now for what he did.'

Hunter's expression was back to its hard lines of bitterness, his gaze glittering. 'He's the reason I do what I do. He ripped my mother off during the divorce. He hid money in offshore accounts just so he didn't have to provide for us. She had nothing, not even a house to live in or a car to drive. It was despicable, and I swore from the moment their divorce was finalised that I would never allow someone to do that to another person if I could help it.'

Millie felt a new respect for his work ethic. She had to readjust her image of him as a powerhouse lawyer intent on acquiring ridiculous amounts of wealth out of other people's misery to that of a man who sought justice for each and every client who walked in the door. He was driven, focussed, indomitable. The perfect ally in a battle. 'I think it's amazing that you've chosen to work in divorce law because of what happened to your mother and sister and you. Is your sister a lawyer too?'

A screen came down over his eyes and he adjusted the position of his water glass on the table with exaggerated precision. 'No. She's not in employment at the moment.' His voice gave no clue to his feelings regarding his sister's lack of employment but there was a muscle in the lower quadrant of his jaw that tap-tap-tippity-tapped like a miniature hammer being held by someone with a not-quite-steady hand.

Millie wasn't known by her friends as a sniffer dog for secrets for nothing. Hunter was better than most at keeping his cards close, but she could sense there was more to his sister's situation than he was letting on. Did Emma have mental health issues? Drug or alcohol problems? An eating disorder? Had her father's desertion so young in her life caused her to struggle during school and thus have difficulty finding gainful employment as an adult? Not everyone got a happy childhood, and those that had the more difficult ones often struggled throughout their lives. Millie wanted to press him for more details, but the waiter came with their entrees and the moment was lost.

Instead, she commented on the gorgeous entrees set down before them—she had caramelised scallops with strawberry salsa, Hunter had crispy duck-breast with cherry port sauce. 'Oh, my goodness, look at the sheer artistry of this food. Can you believe how incredibly creative chefs are? It never ceases to amaze me. Every mouthful is like a work of art.'

'They certainly do a good job here,' Hunter said, picking up his fork. 'Have you been to this restaurant before?'

Millie speared a scallop with her fork. 'No, never, but I've heard heaps about it.'

'You said earlier you haven't been out to dinner with a guy for ages,' Hunter said. 'I guess you didn't eat out much with your fiancé before he passed away.'

In spite of the delicious flavours exploding in her mouth, Millie could feel her appetite slipping away and put her fork back down. 'Well, certainly not at places as fancy as this, but sometimes we'd pick up a fast-food meal if Julian was feeling up to it.'

She paused for a beat and went on, 'Chemo kind of ruins one's appetite and even the flavour of food at times. And once Julian lost his hair he was really self-conscious and hated being seen in public without a cap or beanie on.' A tiny sigh escaped her lips before she could stop it. She picked up her fork and speared another scallop. 'It was hard watching him suffer...'

Hunter reached across the table and laid his broad hand over the top of hers, the gentle pressure soothing, comforting. 'It must have been heart-breaking for you. You were childhood sweethearts, right?'

Millie kept her eyes on their joined hands, conscious of the warmth spreading through her skin from his. Conscious of the lies she was feeding him about her relationship with Julian. 'Yes, we met in school. He only lived a couple of streets from my house, so we hung out a lot together as kids. We started officially dating when we were sixteen. He was diagnosed with a brain tumour just before his eighteenth birthday.'

'How tragic.' Hunter's voice was gentle and full of compassion.

'Yes, it was...' Millie flicked a glance his way and, pulling her hand from underneath his, continued, 'He fought it as bravely as he could for six years. Round after round of chemo, so many specialist appointments, long hours on the chemo ward while he had treatment. In and out of hospital when things got bad. I supported him and his mother. I still see her most weeks. She was understandably devastated when he died. He was an only child.'

'His father?'

Millie gave him a speaking look. 'Another one of those deadbeat dads who walked out on his family. He left when Julian was a toddler. Julian had no memory of him at all, which was probably a good thing in the end.'

But because Julian's mother Lena hadn't had a partner to share the emotional load, Millie had had no choice but to continue to offer support and comfort even though it had made her feel terribly conflicted. Julian was an only child and Lena had relied heavily on Millie when things had got tough. They'd become a tag team to help Julian get through the ordeal of his illness. They'd supported each other. They'd cheered the other on when the other one's hopes had faded. They'd stepped up when the other had had to step back. In some ways, Lena had become more of a mother figure to her than her own mother. Millie knew if she'd broken up with Julian, she'd have been breaking up with his mother as well. It had been easier in the end to continue her relationship with Julian, even though for the last couple of years it had felt like an emotional prison from which she might never escape.

Not that she wanted to reveal any of that to Hunter. She had already shared more than she usually did with someone she barely knew.

'Do you see yourself settling down with someone else one day?' Hunter asked after a short silence.

Millie arched her eyebrow in a pointed manner. 'No. Do you see yourself settling down any time soon?'

He gave a crooked smile that didn't make the full distance to his eyes. 'No. The marriage and happy-ever-after thing isn't for me. I see the other side of love and commitment every day at work. It's enough to turn anyone into a hardened cynic.'

'Yes, well, I've seen enough with my mother trying to get away from difficult husbands who say they love her until they hate her,' Millie said with a sigh. 'She found true love once and lost it.'

'A bit like you, then.' His comment startled her, not because it was true but because it was false. His gaze was unwavering, penetrating, making her feel raw and exposed.

Millie looked back at the barely touched food on her plate, her heart thumping, her skin prickling. *You are a fraud. A liar.* The mental accusation was loud and clanging inside her head, making her increasingly uneasy under the piercing scrutiny of Hunter Addison. Could he read her 'tells'? The micro-expressions or tonal qualities she couldn't always control? She forced herself to meet his gaze, schooling her features into a mask. 'What about you? Have you ever been in love?'

His slanted smile was cynical. 'You're very good at deflection, aren't you?'

Millie held his challenging look. 'A simple yes or no will do.'

'No.' His tone couldn't have been more decisive.

'Let me guess—I bet lots of women have fallen in love with you.' Millie held up her fingers in a tallying motion. 'One—you're good-looking. Two—you're rich and successful. Three…' She decided against mentioning anything about his undoubted sexual prowess but could feel herself blushing regardless.

'Three?' he prompted with an arch of a

single ink-black eyebrow, the sardonic smile still in place.

Millie disguised a tight swallow. 'I'm assuming you're a good lover.' Her cheeks were now hot enough to flambé food, her voice betrayingly husky.

His glinting tawny gaze held hers captive. 'I guess there's only one way you'll know for sure.'

The words hung in the silence like a lure, a temptation, a dare.

Millie's heart missed a beat, then another one. She called on every bit of acting ability she had perfected over the last few years to sit coolly composed in her chair. 'In your dreams, Addison.'

CHAPTER FOUR

THE THING WAS, sleeping with Millie *was* exactly what most preoccupied Hunter's mind just lately. He couldn't stop his imagination playing with the idea of kissing the ripe curve of her mouth, trailing his lips over every delectable inch of her body, being *inside* her, feeling her pleasure spasm around him.

Was he so turned on because he hadn't had a lover in the last couple of months? Such a space between hook-ups was a little unusual for him. He had a healthy, some might even say robust, sexual appetite. He enjoyed the human contact; the physical touch and reciprocal pleasure was something he looked forward to on a regular basis.

But, since he had met Millie on that blind date from hell, he had lost interest in anyone other than her. Which was frankly kind of weird, because she wasn't his type. His type played the hook-up game by the rules. Short, satisfying flings that got the job done without anyone's feelings getting hurt. No strings, no promises, no expectations other than a good time—it could have been his personal tagline.

But something about Millie Donnelly-Clarke with her feisty spirit and constant push-back excited him in a way he had never been excited before. He understood the word no when he heard it. He wasn't so egotistical that he couldn't accept when a woman wasn't interested in him.

But the question of why Millie kept staring at his mouth and blushing begged an answer. An answer he was determined to get one way or the other.

'What? You can't see yourself having a fling with me?' Hunter asked with a teasing smile.

Her cheeks were a rosy pink, her blue-grey gaze flashing with defiance. 'No. I cannot.' Her tone had a hint of starchy schoolmistress about it, but her gaze drifted to his mouth once more, as if pulled by a force outside of her control, and her throat rose and fell over a tiny swallow.

'Because you're not ready to move on from your fiancé?'

Her chin came up another imperious notch. 'Isn't it a little tricky for you, getting involved with a client?'

Hunter held her gaze. 'Ah, but you're not my client. Your mother is.'

Millie's expression faltered for a nanosecond and her small white teeth sank into the plump pillow of her lower lip. But then her gaze inched up to his again, her gaze clear and direct. 'I wouldn't want anything to distract you from doing a good job of sorting out my mother's divorce.'

'I never let my personal life get in the way of my professional one.' Except when it came to Emma. Hunter had lost count of the number of times Emma's issues had impacted on his professional life. He made up for it by working extra hard for his clients when Emma didn't need him so much, but it was there in the background of his mind all the time—the responsibility of making sure all her needs were met, that she was safe and cared for at all times and in all places. That the people taking care of her were trustworthy and dedicated. That no one could hurt her, upset her, frighten her or exploit her.

It was his commitment to his sister.

The only full-time, long-term commitment

he had made so far and was ever likely to make to anyone.

As to being distracted… Well, Millie was the biggest distraction he'd encountered in a very long time, possibly ever.

'So, you're a true workaholic,' Millie said, giving him another uppity glance. 'Work first, play later—if at all.'

Hunter gave an indolent smile. 'Oh, I know how to play, sweetheart.'

Her cheeks darkened to a deep shade of rose. 'One supposes there aren't too many women who ever say no to you.'

'Not many.'

She ran the point of her tongue over her lips and glanced briefly at his mouth before meeting his gaze. 'Will you excuse me? I… erm…need to use the bathroom.' She slipped out of the chair and disappeared through the exit to the conveniences.

Hunter leaned back in his chair and smiled to himself. *You've got this.*

Millie stared at herself in the mirror over the wash basin. Her eyes were overly bright, her cheeks bright-pink, her lips parted as if she had just received a smoking-hot kiss from Hunter's sexy mouth. If she wasn't careful, she would be the next woman who couldn't say no to him.

She slammed her lips together so firmly, they turned white. Why couldn't she handle men like Hunter Addison? Or maybe it was more that she didn't know how to handle herself—the unfamiliar urges and desires triggered by his attention. How was she going to navigate her way through this? She needed him professionally, but her body decided it needed him personally. *Intimately.*

She drew in a ragged breath and finger-combed her hair, the tiny glint of her engagement ring catching the light from above. She lowered her hand and curled it into a fist, her right hand coming over the top of her left to cover the ring, as if that small diamond was acting as her conscience's critical eye on her behaviour. She slowly removed her right hand from her left and gripped the edge of the basin instead.

You have to resist him. You have to.

Millie straightened her shoulders, tossed back her hair and put her game face back on. When she got back to the table, Hunter was wearing his reading glasses and checking something on his phone. He looked up and gave a self-deprecating smile, put his phone down. 'I know. Bad habit. Phones and restaurants don't mix.'

Millie slid back into her seat and flicked her napkin across her lap. 'It's hard, though, isn't it? I'm always on mine.'

'That reminds me…' He picked up his phone again. 'You didn't give me your mother's mobile number or email address. I'll need to give it to Matteo Vitale, the forensic accountant, as he'll want to deal directly with her at some stage.' His fingers were poised over the keys ready to add her mother's details to his contacts.

Details that didn't exist.

Millie swallowed, her heart suddenly racing. 'Erm…she doesn't have one at the moment.'

His eyebrows came together in a frown. 'Then when will she have one, do you think?' There was something a little too lawyer-ish in his tone, bordering on interrogation.

'I'm…not sure. She's not a fan of them.'

'Okay, so how about an email address? She has one of those, I presume?'

She shook her head, her gaze not quite meeting his. 'No email address. You can send any official stuff to my email address or call her on her landline.'

His frown was now so deep it carved a trench between his eyes. 'No email address? You're kidding me, right?'

She briefly met his incredulous gaze before lowering her eyes once more. 'I'm not kidding.'

The silence was so thick she could almost feel it pressing against her chest like a giant hand.

Hunter put his phone back on the table next to his plate with a soft little thud. 'Okay.' He took his glasses off and slipped them into his top pocket. 'So, do you want to tell me what you should have told me before we had the meeting this morning? Or shall I tell you what I think is the problem?'

Millie slowly brought her gaze back to his. 'You've guessed?'

'Your mother has literacy issues.'

Hearing him say it, knowing he had discovered it himself, gave Millie the freedom to nod her head. 'My mother has serious dyslexia. She is functionally illiterate and innumerate.'

'Right, well, it seems my concerns over her finances were well-founded.' He released a long breath and added, 'Look—I wish you'd given me the heads up on it. How does she feel about it? Is she comfortable talking about it?'

Millie gave him a wry look. 'If she was comfortable about it, I would have told you.' She bit her lip and went on, 'I've never told anyone about this before. She's deeply ashamed and embarrassed, and I do everything I can to help her so she doesn't have to feel bad about something she can't help.'

'That must have been tough on you growing up.' His tone was disarmingly gentle, his expression full of empathy.

Millie shrugged one shoulder. 'I managed.'

'Do you have any half-siblings?'

'No, there's just me.'

'Hey. Look at me.' His voice had a commanding edge, but it was tempered by a low, husky note that dismantled another piece of her emotional armour. She had told him the truth about her mother's problem. Why not tell him how it impacted *her*? What had she got to lose?

Millie inched her gaze back up to his. 'I don't expect you to understand. Most people have no idea what it's like to have such a disability. They think she's dumb, but she's not. She's got so much potential, but she can't access it. The modern world isn't set up for people with literacy and numeracy problems. It's incredibly isolating for Mum and it's largely why she's in the financial mess she's in. Everyone rips her off. She gets exploited by husbands, and even her housekeepers at times. I do everything I can to help her, but it's not enough, not now my own business needs more and more of my time.'

By saying it out loud for the first time to another adult, she suddenly realised how much of a burden she'd been carrying—alone. The weight of it was oppressive. It impacted every part of her life. She loved her mum. Would do anything for her mum. But her mum couldn't always be a mum to her. Their places had switched a long time ago—Millie was the adult and her mother the child.

'I know you probably think I can't possibly understand but, believe me, I do,' Hunter said. 'I'll do everything in my power to help your mother. People like her are particularly vulnerable to financial abuse.'

'Thank you.' Millie could barely get her voice to work.

He reached across the table for her hand and, with only a moment's hesitation, she slipped hers into the warm, strong cage of his. His eyes held hers in a lock that made something in her belly wobble. He gave her hand a gentle squeeze. 'It's been a long day. Let's get you home.'

They didn't speak much on the way back to Millie's flat. She got the feeling he was mulling over what she had revealed to him. Every time she glanced at him, he was frowning in concentration. Perhaps he was planning his course of action for her mother's divorce now he had this new information. Millie wished now that she had told him from the outset, but then what if he hadn't offered to help her mother? She'd been walking a fine line with him anyway, given their blighted first date. She wasn't used to being so open with someone. Even her two closest friends knew nothing about her mother's problems. Why had she spilled all to Hunter Addison, of all people?

You didn't spill all. He worked it out for himself.

That was all well and good, but what if his perpetual frown was because he was changing his mind about acting for her mother? Maybe he thought it was too difficult, given her mother's disability. Too complicated and messy. Millie was already risking a lot financially—the divorce process could string out for months and months. How on earth could she ever afford to pay her mother's legal bills?

Hunter pulled up in a space in front of her flat and turned off the engine. He swivelled in his seat to look at Millie. 'Given what you've told me tonight, I think—'

'Don't say it,' Millie interjected, casting a cynical look in his direction before turning to face the front. 'I get it, I really do.'

'What did you think I was going to say?' She could hear the frown in his voice.

Millie glanced at him. 'You think I should get another lawyer to act for my mother.'

Hunter placed a gentle hand beneath her chin and turned her head to face him. He held her gaze for a pulsing moment. 'And why would I want you to do that?' The streetlight outside the car was reflected in his eyes, making them even more heart-stoppingly attractive.

She ran the point of her tongue over her dry lips, her eyes drifting to his mouth. 'Because…because…her situation is too difficult. And it's going to cost a bomb to fix it—if it can be fixed, that is.'

He bumped up her chin with one finger, meshing his gaze with hers. Something tumbled off a high shelf in her stomach and a whole flock of insects fluttered around her heart. 'Something you need to know about me, sweetheart. I thrive on a challenge. The more difficult, the better.' His voice contained a thread of steel, his gaze a glint of delight, his mouth a tempting curve. But somehow, right then, she didn't think he was just talking about her mother's situation.

Millie couldn't stop looking at his mouth, her gaze drawn to it with a magnetic force so powerful, it overruled her resolve to keep her distance. His evening shadow had thickened even in the couple of hours they had spent together.

Spent together. The words were faintly shocking. She had spent the evening with a man she had only met a couple of times. A man she was fiercely attracted to in ways she had never been attracted to in anyone else before. Erotic, primal ways that pulsated in her body whenever she was with him.

Hunter leaned closer, his head coming down as if in slow motion, his mouth so close to hers she could feel the soft waft of his breath against her lips. 'I want to kiss you, but I'm not sure it's worth the risk.' His voice was both smooth and rough honey poured over gravel.

'W-what do you think will happen?' Millie was shocked at the sound of her own voice— whisper-soft, breathless with anticipatory excitement. Breathless with lust.

He nudged one side of her mouth with his lips, just a gentle bump of flesh on flesh, and yet it created a storm of sensation. Tingles, fizzes, darts of need that travelled straight to her core. His lemony aftershave intoxicated her senses. She felt tipsy—no, flat-out drunk and out of control. 'Well, let's see… One: you might slap my face.'

'I abhor violence of any type.' Who was this person sitting in the car with him, almost kissing him? Acting coy and coquettish, as if she had written the handbook on flirting?

'Two: you might kiss me back.'

Millie double-blinked. 'And th-that would be a problem?'

He smiled against the side of her mouth and a wave of incendiary heat coursed through her body. The slight rasp of his stubble made every female hormone in her body throb with pleasure and she wondered what it would feel like against her more intimate flesh. 'For me, yes.'

'W-why?' Her voice wobbled again, her

senses reeling at his closeness, at his smell and touch and overwhelming maleness.

His mouth hovered above hers once more, his warm breath mingling with hers. 'I might not want to stop kissing you.' He trailed his lips over her face to the highest point of her cheekbone, just below her left eye, her skin erupting in tingles of pleasure.

'I—I'm sure you have much better self-control than that…' Millie was surprised she could still get her voice to work, let alone string a reasonably cogent sentence together.

He brushed his lips against her eyebrow and a shower of sensations shimmied down her spine. 'It's not my self-control I'm worried about.' His tone was lightly teasing, so too the gleaming light in his eyes.

Millie raised her eyebrows as though she were auditioning for a role as an affronted spinster in a period drama. It was high time his monumental ego got a slap down. 'What? You think I can't resist you?'

His lazy smile tilted even further. 'There's only one way to find out.'

She hoisted her chin. 'Is that a dare?'

His eyes held hers, then dipped to her mouth. 'Damn right it is.'

Millie stared at his mouth with her heart

thudding so loudly she was sure he would
hear it. The desire to kiss him was so strong,
so tempting, it overrode every reason why she
shouldn't feed his ego by proving him right.

But then, what if she proved him wrong?
What if she kissed him and didn't respond at
all? She could take her mind elsewhere, as
she used to do sometimes with Julian.

She met Hunter's gaze with fortitude. 'All
right. One kiss, and I start it and I finish it.
Okay?'

Was that a glint of victory in his eyes or
something else? Something much more dangerous to her self-control—raw, male desire.
'Done deal.'

Millie leaned closer, determined that only
her lips would be in contact with his and no
other part of his body. She placed her lips
on his in a feather-soft touch before lifting
off again. His drier lips clung to hers as she
pulled away, as if calling her back, and she
curled her hands into fists to stop herself pulling his head down to kiss him the way she
really wanted to. The way her body was de-
manding she kiss him.

'Is that the best you can do?' He placed
a fingertip on her lower lip, idly stroking it
back and forth, back and forth, until every

nerve was tingling. His tone was teasing, his look challenging, and her pulse went haywire.

'We agreed on one kiss.'

One of his hands slid up under her hair and cupped the back of her head, making her scalp prickle with delight. 'That wasn't a kiss according to my standards.'

Millie could only imagine his standards. Sensual, scorching-hot, sexy. She knew she was drifting into dangerous territory by not pulling out of his hold but she couldn't seem to get her self-control back on duty. The sensation of his large hand cupping the back of her head sent waves of pleasure through her body.

'I'm not sure I'm ready for this...' It was a coward's way out, but she used it anyway. She was frightened of the passion he stirred in her. Passion she hadn't experienced in her life before. Passion she wasn't sure she could control if she allowed it off the leash even momentarily.

Hunter picked up her left hand, his thumb slowly rolling over the diamond on her ring finger. 'Because of your late fiancé?'

Millie swallowed and looked down at their joined hands. 'I've never kissed anyone but Julian...'

He let go of her hand and inched up her chin, locking his gaze on hers. 'You wouldn't be betraying him, Millie. You have the right to move on with your life.'

Millie half-lowered her lashes over her eyes, worried he would see the truth she was trying to hide. 'Thank you for a nice evening. I'd better go in now.' She made a move for the door, but he put a hand on her arm and turned her back to face him.

'I want to see you again.' It was a command rather than a request.

'I guess you'll see me at the next meeting in your office with my mother.' Millie kept her tone cool and composed but inside she was trembling with excitement. Forbidden excitement she *must* and *would* control.

He traced a fingertip around her mouth in a slow-motion movement that sent a shower of sparks through her tender flesh. 'I didn't tell you my number three.'

Millie frowned in confusion. 'Number three?'

He gave a slanted smile. 'My third risk-assessment reason for deciding whether or not to kiss you.'

She glanced at his mouth before she could stop herself. 'What is it?'

He lightly tapped the end of her nose with his finger. 'I'll tell you when we next have dinner. I'll pick you up on Friday night, same time.'

'But what if I don't want to have dinner with you?' The truth was, she did want to have dinner with him again. He was the most intriguing and yet infuriating man she had ever met. Infuriatingly attractive.

He cocked one sardonic eyebrow. 'Then you'll never know my third reason.'

Millie gave him a quelling look. 'You're very smooth, aren't you? Do you ever not get your way?'

'Occasionally.' He flashed her another smile and opened his door to get out of the car and walk her to the door, adding, 'But it sure is fun when I meet a little resistance. Makes me all the more ruthlessly determined.'

CHAPTER FIVE

ZOEY, MILLIE'S OTHER FLATMATE, was curled up on the sofa watching a movie when Millie came in after Hunter had walked her to the door. He didn't ask to come in, nor did she invite him, but she was seriously tempted. The only thing stopping her was seeing the light on, signalling her flatmate was home. Zoey clicked the pause button and got off the sofa. 'How was your date with Hunter Addison? I hope it was an improvement on the last time.'

Millie rolled her eyes. 'It wasn't a date. It was just dinner to discuss my mother's divorce.'

'Was your mother there too?'

'No.'

Zoey folded her arms and angled her right hip in an 'I'm older and wiser than you' pose. 'Then it was a date. Did he kiss you?'

Millie could feel her cheeks heating and

turned away to the small kitchen to get a glass of water. 'What makes you think that?' She reached up for a glass and then took it to the sink to fill it from the tap.

Zoey padded across the floor to join her. 'Hello? You're gorgeous and single, and he's gorgeous and single, and you spent the evening together. And I took a peek out of the window and saw you practically sitting on his lap in his car.'

Millie turned off the tap and faced her friend. 'I was not!'

Zoey's eyes danced. 'Look at you, getting all defensive. Did he kiss you? Go on, tell me.'

Millie let out a long breath. 'Actually, I kissed him. But only a little peck on the lips, nothing else.'

Zoey's eyes widened. 'No way. Really? You made the first move? Good on you.'

Millie took a sip of water and then put the glass down on the counter with a little thud. 'He dared me to.'

Zoey's expression was a picture of intrigue. 'Oh, really? Gosh, this is way better than that movie I was watching. Tell me everything.'

Millie frowned and speared one of her hands through her hair and let out another sigh. 'He's the most infuriating men I've ever met. I can't believe he got me to agree to another dinner date with him.'

Zoey gave a tinkle of laughter. 'You do look in the mirror occasionally, don't you? No man worth his testosterone could resist asking you out. But I have to say, Hunter must be pretty damn good at the dating game if he got you to agree. Heaps of guys have been asking you for close on three years and you've always said no.'

Millie bit down on her lower lip and picked at a chipped edge on the counter-top with one finger. 'I'm not sure Hunter is the sort of man I should encourage.'

'Why?'

Her hand fell away from the counter-top. 'He's very…experienced.'

'So? You don't want to be in bed with someone who doesn't know his way around a woman's body. He might be just the thing you need to kick-start your dating life once more.'

'But I never really had a dating life in the first place,' Millie said, perching on one of the kitchen stools. 'Jules and I kind of drifted together rather than dated. We were friends for years and then became lovers and, well, you know the rest.'

Zoey came closer and touched Millie on the shoulder. 'Hey, I know Jules getting sick like that really sucked. It was so unfair when you had your future together all planned. But he died while still loving you. You were by his bedside and holding his hand when he left this earth. It's tragic but somehow special that he died feeling totally secure in your love.'

But Millie hadn't been in love with him. She had silently dreaded it as each day had drawn closer and closer to their wedding date. She had felt so trapped, so imprisoned by her inability to let Julian know she loved him as a friend, not as a life partner.

And she was still imprisoned by her web of lies, unable to move on with her life, still trapped and feeling horribly claustrophobic.

Millie couldn't meet her friend's gaze. 'I know...'

Zoey sighed and reached for a mug off a shelf above the counter. 'At least most of your memories are good ones, I mean, before Jules got sick, that is. What do I have after Rupert did the dirty on me?'

She put the mug down on the counter-top like she was slamming it down on her ex's head, her expression so sour it could have curdled milk. Long-life milk. 'What he did tainted every memory of our time together. I can't even look at photos of us now without wondering how many other women he slept with behind my back. And, worse, how did I not know until I finally stumbled upon his latest squeeze in *our* bed? *Urgh*.'

Millie grimaced in sympathy. 'I can only imagine how devastated you must have felt. But not all men are like that. Maybe you'll find someone who is loyal and fall madly in love with—'

'Oh, no.' Zoey waved her hands in front of her body in a criss-cross motion, in a *no way is that ever going to happen* gesture. 'I am never going to fall in love again. It's not worth the pain. From now on, I'm going to be head girl of the "single and loving it" club.'

'And are you loving it? Being single, I mean?'

Zoey gave her a hooded look and reached for a tea bag from a canister on the counter. 'I'm working on it.'

Hunter drove home from Millie's flat with a smile on his face. What was it about her that made him so energised? So turned on? If it had been one of his usual dates, he would have been in bed with her now. But nothing about Millie was run-of-the-mill. She was captivating, intriguing and so damn gorgeous, he wanted to break his three-date rule.

But hey, he *was* breaking his three-date rule.

Normally, he didn't stay with a lover more than a night or two. He didn't want or need the complications of a longer term relationship. His responsibilities for his sister precluded him from investing in anything other than short-term hook-ups. He knew from experience that most women didn't like taking second place. And any lover of his would have to take second or even third place, when it came to Emma and his career.

But Millie fascinated him, and he couldn't wait to see her again. He wanted to feel her lips on his again—not in that light-as-air way but with full-on passion. He knew she was more than capable of it. He saw it in her eyes, felt it like an electric energy charging the air. She wanted him but was resisting him out of some sense of loyalty to her dead fiancé.

Was it love that held her back or something else?

But there was another reason he wanted to see Millie again. He was determined to get justice for her mother Eleanora, who reminded him so much of his own mother. It churned his gut to see how badly she had been treated, exploited by every husband, this latest one by far the worst. It could take months to uncover the fraudulent behaviour of her husband and that would come at a cost. A cost Millie was paying on behalf of her mother. Hunter wasn't going to see Millie go under financially. He had plenty of money. He didn't need her to go bankrupt to pay him. He regularly did pro bono work. Of course, he didn't broadcast it too widely, in case everyone expected it. But now and again a case would come along, it would light a fire in his belly and he would give it his all.

And this case had created an inferno.

Millie was trying not to count the days until her next 'date' with Hunter. She was in her studio working on some new designs on Thursday afternoon when her assistant Harriet came in from the shop front. 'Someone here to see you, Millie.'

'Who is it?'

'That hotshot lawyer guy—Hunter Addison,' she said, and then added in a stage whisper whilst pretending to fan her face, 'Oh, my goodness, he's gorgeous!'

Millie put down her flat-nosed pliers and rose from her chair. 'Send him in.' She could only imagine what her assistant would make of Hunter coming to visit her. Harriet, just like everyone else in her life, was keen for her to go out more. But was going out with Hunter going to do more harm than good?

Hunter came into her studio, having to lower his head to get through the doorway. 'Hard at work?' he asked with a smile.

'Always.'

He placed a hand on his chest. 'Ah, a girl after my own heart.'

Millie gave him a quelling look. 'I don't think so.'

He came further into the room and the space shrunk as if it had turned into a shoe-box. A child's shoebox. He looked down at the piece she was working on—a bespoke diamond engagement-and-wedding ring ensemble for a client. 'Nice. I had no idea you were so talented.'

'Thank you. I guess you'll know where to come now if you ever find yourself in the market for an engagement or wedding ring.'

He gave a deep chuckle of wry laughter. 'Unless I undergo some sort of personality bypass, that is not going to happen.'

Millie lifted her chin a fraction, her gaze steady on his. 'Never say never.'

Hunter's eyes darkened and her heart skipped a beat. 'Right back at you, sweetheart.'

She frowned. 'What's that supposed to mean?'

He took another step closer, so close she could see every black pinpoint of the stubble peppering his jawline, and every fine line and crease on his sensual lips. Lips she had ever so briefly touched with her own and ever since had wished she had not lifted them off so quickly.

'What are you doing tonight?' he asked.

If Millie lifted her chin any higher she was going to fall over backwards. What was it about his arrogant confidence that infuriated her so much? 'Why?'

'I want to see you.' His gaze flicked to her mouth. 'I have something I want to discuss with you. I decided I couldn't wait until tomorrow.'

'Don't you know that patience is a virtue?'

He gave a devilish grin that made him look even more dangerously attractive. 'I'm afraid I don't have too many virtues, only vices.'

'I can only imagine what they might be.' Her tone was straight out of a nineteenth-century Sunday School room. But nothing in her body felt as prim as her tone. Molten heat was pouring into all her secret places, flames of heat licking at her flesh, ignited by the glint in his gaze.

Hunter sent an idle finger down the curve of her hot cheek. 'I have this irresistible urge to kiss you.' His voice dropped to a deep burr of sound that made the base of her spine fizz.

'I'm not sure that's such a great idea right now…' Millie's heart was beating so hard and so fast, it felt as though she was having some sort of medical crisis. Hunter kissing her might not be a great idea, but it was what she desperately wanted. But admitting it to him would come at the cost of her pride. 'I—I'm at work and my assistant could come in and—'

'So, we'll lock the door.' He took the couple of strides back to the door and clicked the lock into place, the sound in the silence like a gunshot. 'See? Problem solved.'

Millie had a feeling her problems were only just beginning. 'I kissed you the other day and—'

'That wasn't a kiss.' He took her by the upper arms in a passionate hold straight out of a nineteen-fifties Hollywood movie. 'This is a kiss.' And then his mouth came down on hers.

Millie was not prepared for the inferno of lust that slammed into her body as soon as his mouth connected with hers. Her lips moulded to his as if fashioned specifically for him. His lips were firm, hard and insistent, and yet gently persuasive too. He angled his head to deepen the kiss, a low, deep groan coming from the back of his throat. She opened her mouth on a breathless gasp to the commanding stroke of his tongue, her senses whirling as potent heat shot through her entire body.

He crushed her against him, his arms winding around her so there was nothing between them but their clothes. And even through their clothes she could feel the urgent rise of his body against hers. Her own body was responding with primal instinct, melting, liquefying, yielding. His mouth continued its sensual exploration of hers, fuelling her desire to a level she had never experienced before. Hot, urgent, pounding desire that raced through her body with an ache that was part pleasure, part pain. Both extreme tantalisation and exquisite torture.

Hunter loosened his hold and brought his hands up to cradle her face, his mouth still clamped to hers as if he couldn't bear to be away from it. Millie returned his kiss with equal passion, hungry for the taste and texture of his mouth, greedy for the heightening of her senses that drove every thought out of her head other than how much she wanted him. He changed position again, releasing another guttural groan as his tongue mated with hers in a dance as old as time. Desire travelled in a lightning-fast streak up and down her spine, smouldering in a pool of liquid fire between her legs.

She had never been so aroused.

Never been so turned on by a kiss.

Never wanted someone so much it felt like a pain she would do anything to assuage.

Hunter fisted one of his hands in her hair, his mouth moving with hers in an explosively hot exchange of need. Need she could feel pounding in his body where it pressed so shockingly, intimately against hers. The same need she could feel in her own body, the low, dragging ache, the tension of inner muscles, the dewy heat of lust.

He finally dragged his mouth off hers, his breathing as erratic as her own, his eyes glazed with desire. 'So, that clears up that, then.'

Millie tried to disguise the way he had completely ambushed her senses by retreating into a cool mask of indifference. 'Clears what up?'

He smiled and traced around her mouth with a lazy finger. 'You want me so bad.'

She batted his hand away as if it were an annoying insect, frowning for good measure. 'It was just a kiss, Addison. Nothing else.'

'Ah, yes, but what a kiss.'

Millie folded her arms across her body— her traitorous body, her still aching with lust—and cast him another look cold enough to mess with the air-conditioning thermostat on the wall. 'I know what you're trying to do.'

'What am I trying to do?'

'You see me as a challenge.'

'You're definitely that but a delightfully entertaining one.'

Millie turned away before she was tempted to fling herself back into his arms. She went back behind her work bench, using it as a barricade. 'You said you had something to discuss with me. Is it to do with Mum's situation?'

He straightened one of the cuffs of his business shirt. 'I have a proposition to put to you.'

Millie held his smouldering gaze with her frosty one. 'I hope it's not an indecent one?'

Seriously, she could have been transported from a Victorian ladies' college.

The atmosphere began to throb with tension. Erotic tension that made her skin tighten all over and her heart rate spike.

Hunter smiled an enigmatic smile and picked up her jeweller's saw from the work bench and ran his fingertips slowly over the row of teeth. After a brief moment, he put the tool down again and met her gaze with his inscrutable one. 'I've decided to do your mother's divorce pro bono.'

Millie rapid-blinked and her heart missed a beat. 'Why on earth would you do that?' Suspicion was ripe in her tone.

He gave a rueful smile. 'Not for the reasons you're thinking.'

Her chin came up a fraction. 'How do you know what I'm thinking?' She was thinking how wonderful it would be if she didn't have to pay thousands of pounds in legal fees. Pounds she could ill afford.

But she was also thinking, *What does Hunter want in return?*

And, worse, how was she ever going to find the willpower to say no to him?

Hunter's eyes moved back and forth between each of hers in an unnervingly assessing manner. 'You have very expressive eyes and they're not always in agreement with what you say.'

Millie looked away, worried he was seeing far more than she wanted him to. 'It's a very generous offer but I'm afraid I can't accept it. It would...complicate things.'

'How?'

She brought her gaze back to his. 'You know how.'

He arched one eyebrow, one side of his mouth lifting in a lopsided smile. 'You really do have an appalling opinion of my character, don't you?'

'I speak as I find.'

'Let me assure you, I don't need to resort to blackmail to get a woman to sleep with me.'

Millie couldn't drag her eyes away from the shape of his mouth. She could still taste him on her lips—the salty tang that was as addictive as a drug. 'I—I don't understand why you'd make such an offer to go pro bono if you didn't want something in return.'

'Suffice it to say, I feel sorry for your mother.' He scraped a hand through his hair and gave a rough-edged sigh. 'She reminds me of my mother. Gentle, sweet, trusting, naïve. I hate seeing people like that get done over. It's highly likely it will take quite some time to uncover all the funds that have been siphoned off, and that is extremely costly.'

Millie searched his gaze for a long moment. 'But what about the forensic accountant you mentioned? We'll have to pay him, won't we?'

'I've already spoken to Matteo about it. He's happy to go pro bono too.'

Millie chewed at her lip, torn between wanting to howl with relief and throwing her arms around Hunter to thank him. 'I don't know what to say...'

He came round her side of the work bench and placed his hands on the tops of her shoulders. 'Hey, you're not going to go all weepy on me, are you?'

She gave a tremulous smile. 'I might...' She brushed the back of her hand across her right cheek. 'But I should warn you, I'm a messy crier.'

He brushed the pad of his thumb beneath her left eye where a couple of tears had leaked out despite her best efforts, his gaze warm. 'I'm used to it. My sister is the highly emotional type. Cries at commercials featuring puppies or kittens or babies. Drives me nuts.

Not to mention costing me a fortune in tissues.'

'She sounds like a really nice person.'

And so do you... Millie wanted to add, but stopped herself just in time. She couldn't allow herself to *like* him…could she?

Hunter's hands came away from her shoulders and a mask dropped down over his features, as if he regretted talking about his sister. It intrigued her as to why. He sounded as if he really cared about Emma. And why was he the one paying for her tissues? Why would he not want to talk about her? What was going on in Emma's life that made it difficult for him to be open about her?

'What time are you wrapping up here?' Hunter waved a hand towards her workbench, his business-like tone so different from only moments ago.

Millie glanced at the clock on the wall. 'Gosh, is that the time? Harriet was meant to leave half an hour ago.'

Hunter moved across to unlock the door. He undid the lock and asked over his shoulder, 'Dinner tonight? I'll pick you up at the same time.'

'Why don't you let me cook you dinner? I mean, as a thank you.' The invitation was out before Millie could monitor her tongue. What was she thinking, asking him back to her flat when it was likely Zoey would be home? Not only that, her flat was hardly penthouse material, and she was pretty sure Hunter Addison was the penthouse-residing type. Besides, he was used to fine dining in fancy restaurants. How gauche and unsophisticated of her to offer him a home-cooked meal.

'How about we both cook dinner? At my place.'

'That would be…fun, thank you.'

Fun? Don't you mean flipping dangerous? At least if they had gone to her flat she would have had safety in numbers with Zoey there. Not that she could always rely on Zoey being there, as she was often away on advertising business with her father.

But maybe it was better to see Hunter out of the public eye. He attracted a fair bit of press attention and was often photographed with his latest lover. How would Julian's mother feel to see Millie gallivanting around town with an out-and-out playboy?

'I'll organise mains—you do dessert,' he said. 'How does that sound?'

'Sounds like a plan.'

He opened the door and Harriet almost

tumbled in, as if she'd been listening at the door, her face going beetroot-red. 'Oops, sorry. I just wanted to see if it's okay to go home now?'

Millie nodded. 'Yep. Sorry to hold you up. We had…erm…some business to discuss.'

Hunter winked at Millie. 'Until tonight.' And then, with a flash of a charming smile to the star-struck Harriet, he was gone.

CHAPTER SIX

MILLIE BARELY HAD time to get home and shower and change before Hunter was due to pick her up. She had rushed home via the supermarket and bought fresh raspberries and cream and some hand-made chocolates, her anticipation of the evening ahead rising as every minute passed.

But, just as she was putting the last touches to her make-up, her phone buzzed with a text message. She picked up her phone and read the text from Hunter.

Slight change of plans. Will send a car for you. I have to see someone for half an hour. Sam will take you to my house and let you in. Make yourself at home. Hunter.

Millie quickly texted back.

Do you want to take a rain check?

The three little dots showed he was typing back and within a couple of seconds his reply came through.

Definitely not. :)

She clicked off her phone and finished her make-up, wondering who he was seeing. Her stomach nose-dived. Surely not another woman? A quick little hook-up in case she didn't put out? She bit down on her lip until it hurt. She didn't like to think he was the sort of man to do something like that. The more she got to know him, the more she saw the commendable traits in his character. Yes, he was charming, teasing and playful, but underneath that she could sense he was a deeply loyal and principled man. Why else would he be doing her mother's divorce pro bono?

Hunter checked in on Emma on his way home because Judy, the carer, had phoned him to say Emma was being a little obstreperous. He suspected Emma was probably having trouble adjusting to Rupinder's absence, as she was her favourite carer, and Emma had become rather attached to her. He organised for his handyman-cum-gardener, Sam, to pick up Millie in case visiting Emma took longer than expected, but he didn't tell her he was visiting his sister. He had already told her far more than he would tell anyone. Millie was exactly the sort of person Emma would be drawn to—warm, sweet, compassionate. Emma would fall for her in a heartbeat and then what would he do? The last thing he needed was any more complications in his life.

But his attraction to Millie was already one big complication. He had never felt so drawn to someone before. Not just physically, although that was off the charts, but more a sense that she might be a little difficult to walk away from the way he did so effortlessly with other lovers. Would she agree to a short-term fling? That was also part of the attraction—she resisted him, and it turned him on all the more. Not in a creepy 'I'm going to wear her down' way, but because he was sure, underneath that prim and proper exterior, she was a deeply passionate woman who had locked herself away.

Unfortunately, when Hunter arrived Emma

was in the middle of one of her temper tantrums over some perceived slight by Judy.

'Whoa there, poppet, what's got you all worked up?' he said, crouching down beside her on the floor where she was thrashing about like she was three years old. But in a way, she *was* still three years old. The anguish over that fact never failed to grab him by the guts in a cruel fist. He often wondered who and what Emma could have been if it hadn't been for the genetic mix-up that had happened in utero. And he also wondered in his darkest moments why it had got her and not him. He had dodged a genetic bullet, and a large dose of survivor guilt was the payoff.

Emma lifted her red and tear-stained face off the carpet and pouted. 'Judy won't let me have what I want for supper.'

Hunter stroked her tangled hair back off her face. 'And what do you want for supper, poppet?'

She sniffed and pulled herself up into a sitting position and began to wipe her nose on her sleeve, but Hunter whipped out a tissue just in time—years of practice made him faster than lightning at such tasks. 'Here. Use this.'

Emma took the tissue and blew her nose and hiccoughed a couple of times, and then scrunched up the tissue into a ball in her hand. 'I want chocolate,' she said with a mulish look.

'Em, you can't eat chocolate at every meal.' He'd lost count of the number of times they'd had this conversation. 'Remember what Dr Nazeem said? You have to eat a balanced diet otherwise you'll—'

'But I *want* it!' She howled like a banshee and began to drum her heels on the floor, throwing the used tissue away like a missile.

Hunter took her hands in his and drew her into his chest, holding her securely, rocking her gently to soothe her. 'It's okay, poppet. Let's go for a compromise, okay? You have a little bit of proper supper and then you can have some chocolate for dessert. How does that sound? Fair?'

''Kay…' Emma came out of her hyped-up state as if a magic wand had been waved but Hunter knew it wouldn't last. There would be another day, another time when she would lose it again. It was a knife-edge existence for her carers, as it had been for him and his mother over the years. He sometimes wondered if the stress of caring for Emma was why his mother had not been able to survive her blood cancer. She hadn't had the strength or endurance to cope with the chemo—all her strength and endurance had been used up, worn away by the stress and arduous task of caring for her disabled child. And it made Hunter feel all the more guilty that he hadn't been able to do more to help his mother.

Once Emma was settled with her supper on her lap in front of her favourite children's television show, Hunter took Judy aside. 'Are you okay?'

She gave him a weary smile. 'I'm paid to be okay. And very generously, thanks to you. But how are you?'

How was he? What a question. It was times like this that he wondered how he had managed to build the career he had with the burdens he'd carried over the years. Not that he considered Emma a burden. She was his little sister and he loved her. Besides, he didn't know how long he would have her. The doctors hadn't expected her to live this long with her complex condition. He dreaded the day he would lose her. His life had revolved around taking care of her for so long, he didn't know any other way of living.

Hunter forced his lips into a smile. 'I'm fine, as always.'

I have to be.

* * *

Millie was driven to a three-storey Georgian house in Bloomsbury by a pleasant older gentleman called Sam, who told her he often drove Hunter to and from district courts when the need arose. He also did odd jobs around Hunter's house and garden and his wife, Ada, did the housekeeping. Sam showed her into the house and assured her Hunter wouldn't be too much longer, and informed her Ada had dropped off some things for dinner earlier and had set the table in the dining room.

Once Sam had left, Millie took the things she had bought through to the kitchen, quietly marvelling at how well appointed it was—no less than a chef's dream of a place in which to work. She put the raspberries and cream in the smart fridge and left the chocolates on the acre of island bench.

It was strange to be in a person's house without them being there, especially the first time. She couldn't stop herself from having a little snoop around, looking for clues to the man behind the enigmatic smile. Judging from the contents of his fridge, he was a health-conscious eater. And the clean, streamlined décor hinted at a neat and ordered mind...or maybe a very efficient house-keeper. Or both.

Millie continued her tour to the sitting room, complete with shiny black fireplace and a French carriage clock on the mantel-piece above softly ticking in the background. The sofas were deeply cushioned, and she could imagine curling up there with a good book, a glass of wine and Hunter's arm around her...

She jerked back from her wayward thoughts, shocked at the picture they had con-structed in her brain. A domestically cosy picture that had no chance of ever becom-ing a reality.

Because she didn't want it to...*did she*? And, more to the point, nor did he. He wasn't the sitting-by-the-fireplace-with-the-love-of-his-life type. He was a freedom-loving play-boy who was adamant he would never be tied down by matrimony. She could hardly blame him, given his line of work.

But there had been times just lately when Millie wasn't sure what she wanted any more. Being around Hunter, being kissed by him, had shifted her out of a long period of stasis. A guilt-ridden lockdown of her wants and needs. Needs she had pretended for so long didn't exist. But he had stirred something in her, something that had been asleep for a long time. It was like waking from a coma realising nothing was the same as it had been before. How could it be? She could recall every moment of Hunter's explosively passionate kiss. She could recall the hard press of his aroused body against her. Her body was still agitated, restless, wanting more contact. Needing more contact, like an addict needed another fix.

But it wouldn't do to get addicted to Hunter Addison. He was heartbreaker material and the last thing she needed was her heart smashed to pieces. Launching into an intimate relationship again was definitely not on her agenda. She had done the commitment thing and look how it had turned out. She had been trapped, imprisoned by her own promises, and those chains were still around her to some degree.

But the thought of a fling was tempting... especially with Hunter. Dangerously tempting.

Millie moved to the bookshelves at the back of the room to see what sort of taste he had in literature. There were plenty of crime and thriller novels, many legal texts, and history books and biographies. There was even a row of children's picture books, some of the very same titles she had had as a child. So he was a little bit sentimental, was he? He hadn't thrown out his childhood books. How interesting.

She drew out one of her favourites, flicking through the pages, recalling how she had been the one to read them to her mother, not the other way round. She had even tried to teach her mother to recognise the simple words and sentences, with moderate success. But being able to stumble her way through a kindergarten-age picture book was the limit of her mother's ability. Her mum had missed out on early intervention due to the long denial of Millie's grandparents that anything was wrong. And, of course, her mother had developed numerous cover-up strategies to cope. Pretending she'd left glasses which she didn't possess at home, or had sprained a wrist so she couldn't write—the list went on and on.

Millie slid the book back into place with a sigh. So many things would have been different for her mother if she had been able to learn to read.

She glanced around the room for photos

and spied a couple on a walnut table near the window overlooking the garden. There was one of what appeared to be his mother as a young woman, gorgeous, with dark hair and the same whisky-brown eyes as Hunter. There was another one of him at about age five, proudly cradling a new-born baby—his sister Emma, presumably. There was another one of him when his sister was a toddler—he had his arm around her, and she was looking up at him with adoration, and his smile was just as loving.

Millie traced her finger over Hunter's beaming smile and wondered why he wasn't interested in settling down and having children of his own. She put the photo back down but couldn't help noticing there were none of his father. There was, however, one a little separate from the other photos—Hunter as a young boy with his arm around a shaggy dog, smiling broadly, the dog looking up at him in rapt affection.

The sound of Hunter's firm footfall as he came into the room made her swing round with a gasp. She quickly put down the photo. 'Oh, I didn't hear you come in.' She smoothed her hands down the front of her dress. 'I was, erm, looking at the photos. You were a cute kid. Your sister too.'

He put a hand up to loosen his tie, his expression difficult to read. 'Sorry I kept you waiting. I got held up longer than I expected.'

'No problem.' Would he come over and greet her with a kiss? Why was he keeping his distance and acting so aloof? It made her feel uneasy, as if he was regretting asking her to his house. Or maybe his little meeting with whoever it was had put him off spending the evening with her.

'Would you like a drink before we start on dinner? I got my housekeeper to pick up some things.' His voice was polite but formal and it made her feel as if a chasm had opened up between them. He was on one side, she was on the other. After the scorching kiss they had shared in her studio, it seemed an odd way to behave. Was he regretting kissing her? She could never regret kissing him. She ached to do it again, to feel his mouth moving with such heat and passion against hers.

Millie forced her lips into a smile. 'Why not?'

He opened a cleverly concealed bar fridge and took out a bottle of champagne. 'Since you like a few bubbles in your glass, how about this?'

There were quite a few bubbles fizzing in her bloodstream right now from just being in the same room as him. 'I would love some. I guess this is kind of a celebration, isn't it? Well, for me anyway, given you're not charging any legal fees. I still don't know how to thank you. When I told Mum this afternoon, she burst into tears. She's so terribly grateful, as I am.'

He expertly removed the cork from the bottle with a soft little pop, an enigmatic smile curling the edges of his mouth. 'Everyone deserves a break now and again.' He poured two glasses of champagne and carried them to where she was standing. He handed her one. 'To seeing justice done.'

Millie clinked her glass against his, her eyes unable to move away from the magnetic pull of his gaze. 'Thank you.'

His lips quirked in another fleeting smile, and he tipped his glass back and took a measured sip, but the uneasiness she'd sensed in him was still there. He hid it well, but she could sense it in the way he held himself aloof. He hadn't touched her other than to hand her the glass of champagne, and that seemed odd, given their kiss that afternoon. And he had a faraway look in his eyes that reminded her of the first time they had met. Preoccupied and distant. Brooding.

'Is everything all right?'

He blinked, as if he had forgotten she was there. 'Sorry. What?'

Millie touched him on the arm. 'You seem a little distracted. Are you okay?'

He placed his hand over the top of hers and gave a crooked smile. 'You're the second person to ask me that today. I'm fine.'

'I just thought…after what happened this afternoon in my studio…well, maybe you'd changed your mind about dinner. Or you have other more important things to do.'

He put his glass down and then took hers, setting it down on the table next to them. 'Let's do a replay. I'll come back in and greet you the way I should have the first time.'

Millie watched him stride back to the door of the sitting room, disappearing for a moment outside and then coming back in with a winning smile.

'Hi, honey, I'm home.' He swept her up into his arms and swung her in a full circle, then slid her down his body until she was back on her feet. 'Pleased to see me?'

Clearly *he* was pleased to see *her*. She could feel the proud bulge of his erection pressing against her belly. A shiver passed over her flesh and, on an impulse she couldn't stop in time, she linked her arms around his neck and smiled. 'That's much better.'

'But still needs improvement, right?' He gave her a mock-serious look, his eyes twinkling.

'Depends what you have in mind.' Who knew she could be so flirtatious? And have heaps of fun doing it? Her blood was singing through her veins, her heart hopscotching in her chest.

'Believe me, sweetheart, you do not want to know what's on my mind right now.' His tone was dry, his glinting gaze sending another shiver down her spine and a pool of liquid heat straight to her core.

'Try me and see.'

He pressed a light kiss to her lips and released her, leaving her aching, hungry for more. His gaze lost its playful spark and his expression became full of gravitas. 'There's something I need to make clear. I don't want you to sleep with me out of a sense of gratitude. If we sleep together, I want it to be because you want to have a fling with me as equals, okay?'

A fling. Millie rolled her lips together, suddenly lost for words. He was offering her a fling. A short-term relationship that would satisfy the needs he had awakened in her. Needs she had never felt so powerfully before. A fling was not a long-term commitment, so that would be fine, wouldn't it? Long-term commitment was not her thing any more. No more emotional prisons. No more entrapment. Hunter wanted what she wanted—a short-term fling to explore the passion that had fired up between them.

'I don't know what to say.' She couldn't hold his gaze and looked at the loosened knot of his tie instead. 'It's…tempting…'

'But?'

She brought her eyes back to his. 'I've only had one lover. I have so little experience compared to you. I'll probably disappoint you, or won't excite you enough, and—'

He placed his hands on her hips and drew her back against his hard frame. 'You can already feel how much you excite me.'

She gave a gulping swallow, her legs trembling with desire so hot and strong, it threatened to engulf her. 'I—I can't imagine why you'd be excited by someone like me.'

He smiled and brought his mouth down close to hers. 'Everything about you excites me. You're funny and cute and whip-smart. And I like how you stand up to me. It turns me on big time.'

Millie breathed in the scent of him, the male musk and expensive citrus notes that intoxicated her senses into a stupor. She was under some sort of magical spell, turning into a wanton woman with no other motivation other than to get her physical needs met. And sooner rather than later. She wanted to say yes. She ached to say yes. Every female hormone in her body was screaming, *say yes!*

But there were other things to consider, other people's feelings to take into account. Lena, for instance. How could Millie have a full-on and very public fling with Hunter Addison without hurting her? And there were her own feelings to consider. Hunter was a heart-stoppingly attractive man with so many wonderful qualities. What if she were to lose her heart to him? He wasn't interested in anything long-term. A fling was what he was offering. She had only ever been in a long-term and totally committed relationship—so committed she was still in it in a sense, because that was what others thought. She had encouraged them think it.

'Hunter…there's something I need to tell you…' She glanced down at the engagement ring on her hand.

He placed his hand over her left one, his expression sombre. 'I can only imagine how hard it must be to move on from the love of your life. But it's been three years. Do you think he would have waited as long as that?'

Millie sucked part of her lower lip into her mouth, her mind spooling back to the last words Julian had said to her. *I will love you for ever.*

She lifted her gaze back up to Hunter's. 'It's not what you think… *I'm* not what you think.' She took a ragged breath and continued, 'I fell out of love with Julian years before he died. I—I didn't have the heart to tell him. He was devastated enough over the prognosis. He had a really difficult to treat form of brain cancer. The first surgery changed him. When he woke from the induced coma they had him in for a few days post-op, he wasn't the person I used to love. I kept hoping the old Jules would come back but he never did. But he needed me, and I stayed.'

Hunter frowned darkly. 'Oh, you poor, sweet darling.' His arms came round her and held her close against his chest, one of his hands gently stroking the back of her head. 'I can't imagine how trapped you must have felt.'

Millie glanced up at him through misty eyes. 'It's why I never refer to him as Jules any more, always Julian. The old Jules had gone and nothing I could do could get him back.'

He cradled her face in his hands. 'What you did was brave and honourable and incredibly selfless. But don't you see, it's time to move on? You've made enough sacrifices for Julian. You don't have to beat yourself up over not loving him the way you used to.'

'I feel so ashamed...' She looked at the knob of his Adam's apple rather than meet his gaze. 'Everyone felt so sorry for me when Julian died three days before the wedding. But I was glad I didn't have to take the pretence that far. Glad. Don't you think that's dreadfully shameful of me? To actually be *glad* he died?'

Hunter raised her face so her gaze meshed with his. 'Is that why you still wear his engagement ring? As a form of self-flagellation?'

Millie bit her lip and nodded. 'I've spent the last three years playing the role of grieving fiancée. Looking back, I guess it was easy enough to act, because I genuinely cared about him as a friend—as indeed I care about lots of people close to me. The irony is, I'm usually hopeless at keeping secrets. I couldn't even keep my friend Ivy's surprise thirtieth birthday party from her, but I've lived this lie for so long, I don't know how to live my life any other way.'

'There is another way,' Hunter said, holding her by the shoulders in a firm but gentle hold. 'You move on. Live your life. Do the things you want to do, things Julian would want you to do. He wouldn't want you throwing your life away. Not the old Jules, anyway, right? The one you loved?'

Millie blinked back tears. How brilliantly he had put it. She was allowing the sick, changed version of Julian to hold her back from living an authentic life. The Jules she had loved would not have wanted her to throw her life away. How had she not realised that until now? 'You're right, but it's still going to be difficult. I might have to feel my way for a bit.'

He smiled and stroked her cheeks with

his thumbs in a slow, spine-tingling caress. 'That's my girl.'

His girl. But for how long? She was a temporary diversion for him, just like all his other lovers. Nothing permanent. No commitment other than the duration of their fling. No sitting by the fireplace in each other's arms for the rest of their lives.

Just for now.

Perfect…wasn't it?

'Don't you mean your girl of the moment?' Millie injected her tone with light playfulness.

Something flickered over his features—a rapid blink, a muscle twitch near his mouth, a slight dimming of his smile. 'There's nothing wrong with living in the moment as long as it's an unforgettable one.' And his mouth came down and set fireworks off in hers.

CHAPTER SEVEN

MILLIE GASPED AS his lips moved against hers with incendiary heat and purpose. Streaks of fire flashed through her body, her growing desire for him leaving her breathless and pliant in his arms. His tongue stroked the seam of her mouth and she opened to him, her lower body going to molten lava as his tongue mated with hers. The flickering movements, the bold thrusts and darts, heated her blood to boiling.

He crushed her to him, his hard body imprinting every soft curve of hers with his unmistakable erotic intent. An erotic intent she welcomed with every cell of her body. Her intimate female flesh tingled and tightened, her breasts aching for his touch. Her breasts suddenly felt too small for her bra—they were straining against the lace barrier, desperate to feel the caress of his hands.

He groaned against her lips, one of his hands sliding up to the nape of her neck, his touch electrifying. 'I want you so damn much. Do you have any idea what you do to me?'

Millie shivered as his mouth blazed a trail of heat from below her ear, over her neck and to the V of her top. 'I want you too.'

And what he did to *her* was a revelation. A spine-tingling, bliss-inducing revelation that shocked her to the core. She hadn't felt anything like this level of desire before. It was all-consuming, taking over mind and body in a storm of heightened sensuality. She was conscious of every movement of his lips against her skin, the cup of his hand at the back of her neck, the stroke of his tongue below her ear, the feather-light caress of his lips on her jawline as he moved down to her chin and back again.

His mouth came back to hers in a deep kiss that made the hairs on her head tingle at the roots and her heart rate escalate. His tongue played with hers in a teasing dance that sent shivers racing down her spine and heat to pool between her thighs. Lava-hot heat that made her limbs tremble like a new-born foal's. She would have fallen if he hadn't been holding her so firmly.

His mouth left hers to move back down her neck, one of his hands pushing aside her top so he could access her décolletage.

'You smell divine…' He breathed in deeply, as if he was taking in an intoxicating vapour. He let his breath out and added, 'I want to taste you all over.' His voice with its husky edge, and his lips with their silken caresses as they moved across her skin, set her flesh alight. She had never felt such powerful sensations moving through her body. He tugged her top out of her skirt and slid a warm hand up to cup a breast still caged in her bra, and she gave a little gasp as a shudder passed through her.

'Oh…oh…'

His hand stilled on her breast, his hooded gaze meeting hers. 'Tell me what you like.'

Millie pushed herself further into his hand, desperate to feel him skin-on-skin. 'I'm still discovering what I like. My erm, preferences weren't always a priority with Julian.'

'You didn't enjoy sex with him?'

She lowered her gaze, unable to meet his searching look. 'Not really… It became a chore, to be honest.'

He stroked his thumb over her tight nipple, the bra still in place, but even through the lace she could feel the tingling sensations in her flesh. 'I want you to enjoy everything we do together.' He tipped up her chin so her gaze meshed with his. 'Hey, don't be shy. It's important you communicate to me what works for you.' He gave a slow, sexy smile and added, 'And, if you don't know it yet, then we can discover it together.'

Millie reached up to stroke his lean jaw, her lower body flush against his, her senses reeling from the close contact. 'That sounds like fun.'

Hunter lowered his head and smiled against her lips. 'It will be.' The confident assurance in his tone sent another shiver coursing down her spine.

Millie opened to him again, her arms winding around his neck, her breasts crushed against his chest, need spiralling through her body. His hands cupped her bottom, holding her tightly against the ridge of his erection, a deep, guttural groan escaping from his lips as he deepened the kiss even further. His tongue teased hers in a cat-and-mouse game that made her pulse race and her heart pound.

After a few breathless moments, he lifted his mouth from hers. 'Let's go upstairs.'

Millie knew by following him upstairs to

his bedroom that she would be stepping over a threshold. Over a threshold to a fling. A short-term affair that had no future. Some of her hesitancy must have shown on her face, for he took her hands in his, his expression etched with lines of concern. 'You're having second thoughts?' he asked gently.

Millie twisted her lips into an almost-smile. 'I want you. I didn't think it was possible to want someone so much…'

'I'm sensing a big "but" coming.'

She released a stuttering sigh. 'This is so… so normal for you. Having sex with someone who catches your eye and moving on when it's over. I don't know how to play this game. I've only been in one relationship. What do I know about having a fling? Nothing.'

Hunter placed his hands on her hips. 'Millie, listen to me. I'm not long-term relationship material. What I'm offering is a short-term fling. No strings, no promises of for ever— just a good time for both of us while it lasts. If you can't accept that, or feel it's too much of a compromise of your values, then we'll go no further.' He spoke as if he was reading out a legal contract. The terms. The points. The clauses.

Millie could feel the searing heat of his

hands on her hips, his hold not quite possessive but not far off. Her body was drawn to
him even as her mind kept raising little red
flags. But he had awakened something inside
her—something that ached and willed her
to step across the threshold and explore the
sensuality he promised in every kiss, every
caress, even in every look of his tawny gaze.
She looked at his mouth, her own mouth aching to feel the firm press of his once more.
'I've never felt so attracted to someone before.' Her gaze lifted to meet his. 'It's kind of
scary, given how much I disliked you when
we first met.'

Hunter stroked her left cheek with a lazy
movement of his thumb, his expression wry.
'Was I that much of a crashing bore that
night?'

Millie linked her arms back around his
neck and raised herself up on tiptoe so her
mouth was within a breath of his. 'If you had
been, maybe I wouldn't be here now wondering if I'm completely out of my mind to accept your offer of a fling.'

His eyes darkened, his breath mingling intimately with hers. 'So, that's a yes?'

She brushed her lips against his in a but-
terfly-light caress. 'It's a yes.'

* * *

Within a few moments, they were upstairs in Hunter's luxuriously appointed bedroom. The king-sized bed would have dominated any other room, but this room had space to spare. Tastefully decorated in white with touches of navy-blue and grey, the room had a masculine feel without it being oppressively so. It made her small bedroom at her flat look like a broom cupboard.

Hunter drew her close to him, his arms going around her body, his look searching. 'Are you sure this is what you want?'

Millie pushed her doubts to the back of her mind, allowing her body to take charge. 'I want you to make love to me.'

His mouth came down to hers in a leisurely kiss, as if to show her he wasn't going to rush her, or perhaps to give her time to change her mind. Millie wasn't going to change her mind—she couldn't. Her need for him was so intense it consumed every part of her body, ripples of clamouring longing coursing through her flesh with increasing force and speed. His mouth moved to her décolletage, his hands gently unbuttoning her top, button by button, the brush of his fingers sending another wave of want through her body.

'You are so beautiful.' His voice was low and deep and rough around the edges, his gaze hungry, dark and glittering with lust.

Millie shivered as her top slipped from her shoulders like sloughed skin. But, instead of feeling embarrassed to be half-naked in front of him, she felt proud, especially when he sucked in a breath and brought one of his hands up to cup her breast. His other hand reached behind her to undo the fastening on her bra and it too slipped to the floor at her feet. He brought his mouth down to her left breast, his tongue circling her nipple, teasing it into an even tighter bud. He took her nipple in his mouth, sucking on her with the gentlest pressure, the sensations rioting through her flesh like tiny starbursts of pleasure.

Hunter moved to her other breast, the slight rasp of his stubble against her sensitive skin sending another wave of delight through her body. 'Everything about you is so damn beautiful.'

'You don't look too bad yourself, but I need to see more of you.'

He gave her a devilish grin and held his arms out wide as an invitation. 'Go for it.'

Millie set to work on his shirt, determined to get her hands on him, needing to feel the warmth of his skin against hers. She managed a couple of the buttons but he helped her with the rest, shrugging off the shirt and tossing it over his shoulder. She placed her mouth on his chest, tasting his salty skin with her lips and tongue, delighting in his swift intake of breath. She kissed her way up to his mouth, relishing the crushing pressure of his lips as he took masterful control. The rest of their clothes were removed in between passionate kisses and fervent caresses.

Millie was a little surprised at how comfortable she was, being completely naked in front of him. It felt the most natural thing in the world to stand before him with his eyes greedily drinking in her feminine form. She glided a hand down his chest to his rock-hard abdomen, her lower body melting with desire to see him so aroused and ready for her.

'Touch me.' It was one-part command, two parts plea, the edge of desperation in his voice thrilling her senses into overdrive.

Millie stroked her fingers over his proud length and he sucked in a breath, as if her touch delighted him as much as his did her. She grew bolder, taking him in her hand and massaging his swollen flesh. 'You're so…

big...' Her voice came out as a breathless whisper.

He cupped her face in his hands and held her gaze with his smouldering one. 'We'll go at your pace, not mine. You are the one in charge, okay?'

'Okay...' Millie couldn't express how touched she was by his assurance, but she tried to show it in how she caressed him. She explored his length with her fingers, circling the head of his erection with her thumb, relishing in his indrawn breaths and shuddering groans. She ached to be joined to him, her body on fire with longing. She removed her hand and pressed her hips against him, delighting in the thickness of his arousal against her belly. 'I want you.'

'Then you shall have me...but first things first.' His sexy drawl and glinting gaze sent a shiver of heat through her body.

He led her to the bed and laid her down, coming down beside her, his hand on her hip. Now it was time for Millie to suck in her breath. His mouth moved down her body, from her breasts to her belly button and then to her mound. She shivered as his lips played with her female flesh in soft little movements, his warm breath skating over her skin.

He parted her folds and tasted her, and she shuddered as tingles of pleasure shot through her body. He continued the sensual caress with increasing speed, ramping up her response to him until she was feverish with the need to let go, but unable to give herself permission. It was so new to her, foreign, and out of her bounds of experience to be so vulnerable in front of a lover.

Hunter lifted his head to look at her. 'Relax into it, don't fight it. Don't be scared of letting go.'

Easy for you to say, Millie thought. He'd probably had dozens of women going down on him. She was an oral-sex virgin. 'I—I don't think I can. I've never done this before...'

His brows came together. 'Never?'

Millie shook her head, a sigh escaping her lips. 'Julian was a bit prudish when it came to the female body.'

Hunter placed one hand on her belly, the other gently brushing the hair back from her forehead, his eyes holding hers in a lock that felt as tender as a caress. 'You're beautiful and taste gorgeous. Let me pleasure you. Don't think, just feel. Promise?'

Millie released a shaky breath. 'Promise.'

He brought his mouth back down to her folds, slowly caressing her with his lips and tongue, exploring her, tasting her, drawing from her a response she hadn't thought herself capable of—a powerful, earth-shattering response that sent shudders of pleasure throughout her body in cascading waves. She heard someone crying out and then realised with a little jolt it was her. She had never made such voluble sounds during sex before, but then, why would she have? She had never felt anything like the pleasure Hunter was evoking in her.

Millie flopped back on the pillows with a breathless sigh. 'Oh, my gosh... Did that really just happen?'

Hunter smiled and stroked the length of her thigh. 'It just did. And I'm going to make it happen again.' He angled himself away for her in order to get a condom out of the drawer beside the bed. He applied it to himself and came back to her, his eyes glittering with lust. 'But remember, you're still in control. If you want to stop at any point, then we can stop.'

Millie pulled him down to her. 'Please make love to me. I want to give you pleasure too.'

Hunter brought his mouth back to hers in a

drugging kiss that made the hairs on her scalp tingle and her desire reignite. His tongue played with hers, calling it into an erotic dance that sent quivers of delight through her body. He positioned himself at her entrance, his muscled thighs entwined with hers, his powerful body poised to take intimate possession. She arched up her pelvis to encourage him, desperate for the connection, hungry for more of his potent passion.

He slid into her body with a deep groan, her body wrapping around him, her senses reeling at the contact. He began a slow rhythm, the friction of their joined bodies sending darting arrows of pleasure through her body. The tension in her intimate muscles grew and grew, the swollen heart of her aching for the release it craved.

Hunter brushed back the hair from her face, his body deep inside her, his eyes locked with hers. 'Am I going too fast?'

Millie pulled his head down so she could access his mouth. 'Not fast enough.'

'Let's see what I can do about that.' The playful edge to his tone was a new experience for her. There had been little playful about sex with her late fiancé. It had been more of a blink-and-you'll-miss-it session in which her needs and pleasure hadn't even been on the agenda.

But with Hunter it was all about her pleasure and needs.

Millie's senses were so heightened, she could feel the cool caress of the cotton sheets against her skin, the exquisite softness of the feather pillow beneath her head, the sensual stroke and glide of his hands on her body and the driving force of his erection sending her senses into a tailspin. He went deeper, harder, faster, his own breathing becoming ragged, his groans of delight thrilling her to the core of her being. Then he slipped a hand between their rocking bodies and caressed her intimately, his touch like magic on her flesh. She soared into another hemisphere, a place of intense physical pleasure that rippled through her in giant coursing waves, leaving no part of her body unaffected.

She was still in the throes of her release when he shattered around her, the shudders of his body sending another wave of pleasure through hers. She held him in her arms during the storm, breathing in the musky scent of their coupling. And then breathing in time with him during the quiet peaceful time afterwards.

Hunter lifted himself up on one elbow, his gaze holding hers in an intimate tether that made her heart kick against her breastbone. 'If I'd known it was going to be as good as that, I would have worked a little harder on that blind date to charm you into my bed then and there.' He gave a rueful grimace. 'What a missed opportunity.'

Millie smiled and traced the contour of his mouth with an idle fingertip. 'You didn't seem to even notice that I was a woman that night. You had a perpetual frown on your face the whole time.'

Something flickered over his features and his eyes dipped to her mouth. 'Yes, well, let's not talk about what a jerk I was that night.'

'Why were you so…so brooding and unfriendly? And don't say it was because I was an absolute cow from the moment we met, because I saw you frowning even before I got to the table.'

He captured her finger and kissed the end of it, his gaze locking with hers. 'You weren't any such thing. I was kicking myself for agreeing to a blind date in the first place, but Beth and Dan were pretty insistent, and caught me at a weak moment.' He gave her hand a tiny squeeze and continued, 'I probably should have cancelled rather than turn up in a foul mood. Forgive me?'

Millie pressed a kiss to his lips. 'Forgiven. But you still haven't told me why you were in such a foul mood. Was it a work thing? I mean, your job must be pretty stressful at times.'

He smiled with his mouth but not with his eyes. 'Something like that.' He dropped a light kiss to her lips. 'Is your work stressful?'

Again Millie idly stroked a finger across his collarbone. 'Now and again I'll get a couple in who can't agree on what they want. But mostly it's great. I love designing. I grew up around diamonds, as my grandfather—my father' father, that is—started the business as a young man. I started making my own jewellery in kindergarten. But pasta tubes and coloured beads are not as exciting as diamonds, I have to say.'

He laughed and picked up her left hand. 'And this?' He rubbed his thumb over her engagement ring. 'Is this one of your designs?'

Millie twisted her mouth and then sighed. 'No. Julian proposed to me a couple of weeks after he was diagnosed with cancer. It caught me completely off-guard. I mean, we were teenagers, and not even thinking about setting down just yet, and then suddenly he's asking me to marry him. I didn't know what to do.'

'So you said yes.' There was no judgement or criticism in his tone, just gentle understanding, and it totally disarmed her.

Millie glanced up to meet his eyes. 'I felt so trapped from the moment he put the ring on my finger. Don't get me wrong, I cared about him, but not enough to marry him. We were only eighteen years old. I found myself playing a role that became increasingly claustrophobic, especially when he changed. He wasn't the same person, but then nor was I.'

Hunter passed the pad of his thumb over the small diamond ring again. 'Why don't you take it off?'

She looked at his thumb moving over the ring and something in her chest tightened. 'I can't get it off now. I'd have to saw it off, and I can't quite bring myself to do it.'

He turned the ring on her finger and tested it against her knuckle but it refused to budge. 'That could be a problem if someone else wants to give you an engagement ring.' His expression was inscrutable, his tone mild.

Millie gave a light laugh. 'That's not going to happen. I'm not interested in settling down again. Been there, done that.'

Hunter tapped her playfully on the tip of her nose. 'See? I told you, you're a girl after my own heart.' He brought his mouth back down to hers in a lingering kiss, his hand stroking up and down the flank of her thigh. After a moment, he broke the kiss to look down at her. 'I never did tell you my number three reason for not kissing you that day in your studio.'

'Oh, yes, that's right. What is it?'

His eyes held hers in a glittering lock. 'Stay here with me tonight.'

Millie raised her brows. 'You mean all night? That's your number three?'

He swept a strand of hair back off her forehead, his expression set in more serious lines. 'I generally don't do sleepovers.'

'But you're making an exception in my case? Why?'

He traced a line down the curve of her cheek, a shutter coming down in his gaze. 'You and I want the same thing—a fling without strings. We both understand what this is and know it can't go any further.'

Did she want the same thing, though? No strings. No promises of 'for ever'. No long-term commitment. Tiny doubts were assembling at the back of her mind, like extras on a theatre set waiting for a call to step on stage. Doubts that lingered in the shadows of her conscience, every now and again drifting into a thin shaft of light.

Millie brought her hand up to his face and trailed her fingers down his stubbled jaw. 'Can we keep our…fling private for now? I mean, I don't want Beth and Dan to get any funny ideas about us. Nor do I want to be painted as your latest squeeze in the press.'

Hunter captured her hand and pressed a kiss to her bent knuckles. 'Fine. But I have the perfect place to take you where we will be entirely alone.'

'Where?'

'I have a private yacht moored in Greece.'

Millie widened her eyes. 'You must have handled a lot of very expensive divorces in your time.'

He gave a crooked smile. 'I was lucky with some investments early in my career.' He released her hand and added, 'Was that your stomach or mine growling for food?'

Millie placed a hand on her empty stomach. 'I think it was mine.'

Hunter swung his legs over the edge of the bed and then held out his hand for her with a wolfish grin. 'Come on. We need our energy levels boosted for what I have mind later.'

A shiver coursed down Millie's spine and she took his hand. 'That sounds…interesting.'

He gathered her close, naked skin to naked skin, and another shiver cascaded over her flesh. 'But first, a little entrée.' He brought his mouth down to hers in a scorching kiss that set her senses on fire.

Millie forgot all about food. All she could think about was the taste and texture of his mouth and the molten heat he evoked in her body. If this was what happened during a fling, then she wanted more of it.

Much more.

CHAPTER EIGHT

ONCE DINNER WAS OVER, Hunter sat with Millie in front of the fireplace in his sitting room, their glasses of wine on the coffee table in front of them. His body was replete with food but hungry again for her. But he was conscious that she hadn't had sex in a long time and too much too soon could be uncomfortable for her.

Her response to him delighted him in ways he could barely describe. He had electric tingles from just having his arm draped across her slim shoulders. His senses were intoxicated by the fragrance of her skin and hair, his body still humming from their explosive love-making before dinner.

You're having a sleepover with her? The voice of his conscience prodded him, but he pointedly ignored it. They were on the same page about their fling. Neither of them wanted anything more than a short-term affair. Millie was still wearing her late fiancé's ring and she had no intention of replacing it with anyone else's.

And Hunter was certainly not going to put one on her finger. A commitment of that sort had been ruled out in his head long ago. It was a decision that was reinforced, confirmed as the right one, every day of his life. He only had to think back to his mother to understand the heartache of lost love. He had no desire to experience it himself or cause someone else to experience it through his actions.

And then, of course, there was Emma.

If he were to marry and have a family of his own, Emma would no longer have full access to him. He would have other priorities, other responsibilities that would have to come first. She hadn't coped when their father had left. How would she cope if Hunter created a new family, even if he did his best to be there for her? Even the most accommodating partner would find the rollercoaster of caring for his sister tiresome.

No. He was fine living his life as he did. He knew how to get his physical needs met without compromising his own or another's interests. He never promised what he knew he couldn't deliver. Unlike his father, who had promised to love and protect his wife and family and then dumped them when things got a little tougher than he'd expected.

One of the things he had never been able to forgive his father for was the loss of his beloved dog Midge. When they had been forced to move into a tiny flat, Midge had had to be rehomed. He could still remember the look of confusion on Midge's face when they'd driven away after dropping her at the rescue shelter. Something had shut down inside him that day, a steel cage going around his heart. He had decided he would not love and lose ever again.

Hunter lifted a hand to Millie's head and threaded his fingers through the silk curtain of her hair. She glanced up at him and smiled, her grey-blue eyes clear and pure. Her beauty at odd moments like these stole his breath clean away. He wasn't so shallow that looks were high up on his list of preferences, but Millie had the whole package—intelligence, looks, a kind nature and the ability to fight from her corner. He found her spirited attitude towards him potently, powerfully attractive.

He placed his hand on the curve of her

cheek and angled her head so he could plant a kiss on her soft mouth. Her lips clung to his, her arms winding around his body, her breathless sigh of encouragement sending a wave of red-hot heat through his pelvis.

He pressed her back down on the sofa, coming over her with his weight propped on one elbow, the other hand stroking the sweet curve of her breast. 'Whose idea was it again to get dressed before dinner?' His tone was lightly teasing.

Her smile made her eyes sparkle like diamonds. 'I'm not used to wandering around naked.' She lifted a hand to his face and traced the outline of his mouth, making his skin tingle and his desire for her to stampede in his blood. 'Maybe you should have a guest bathrobe on hand for your lovers when they sleep over.'

'I'll think about it.' He nibbled on the shell of her ear and she writhed in delight.

'How many have slept over?' There was nothing in her tone to suggest anything but mild interest, but the slight bracing tension in her body was a giveaway.

Hunter meshed his gaze with hers, his hand caressing her breast underneath her top. 'You're the first.' It was true. He hadn't taken this step before. His home was his sanctuary and he didn't want any lovers leaving toothbrushes or toiletries and thinking they had a chance of changing his mind about settling down any time soon.

Millie's brows shot up in surprise. 'Really? So why me?'

He dropped a light kiss to her mouth. 'Someone had to be the first. It might as well be you.'

She tugged at his hair in a playful manner. 'That's not a proper answer. Tell me exactly why you wanted me to stay over tonight.'

Hunter's gaze went to her mouth and another lightning bolt of lust slammed him in the groin. 'Fishing for compliments, Miss Donnelly-Clarke?' He used his court voice.

She arched her brows, her eyes twinkling. 'Evading the truth, Mr Addison?'

The truth was a little too confronting for him to examine it too closely. He pushed it to the back of his mind, unwilling to cast any light on its shadowy presence. He wasn't in any danger of falling for her. His rules were the rules for good reason.

Hunter set to work on unbuttoning her top. 'The truth is, I wanted to get you naked and keep you naked for hours. Any objections?' He uncovered her breast and cradled it in his hand.

Her cheeks flushed with pleasure and she shivered under his touch. 'No objections.'

Millie woke during the night to the sound of a telephone ringing downstairs in the sitting room. She glanced at Hunter, who was sound asleep beside her, one of his strongly muscled legs flung over hers. She knew it wasn't her phone, for she had turned it to silent, and it was in her bag on the floor next to the bed. She nudged him gently. 'Hunter? Is that your phone?'

He sat bolt-upright and lunged for the bedside lamp switch. 'Shoot. I forgot to bring it upstairs.' He swung his legs over the side of the bed, dragged a hand through his hair and stood. 'Go back to sleep. It's probably a prank call anyway. I sometimes get them from an aggrieved ex of a client.' He snatched up his bathrobe and shrugged it on, loosely tying the waist ties as he left the room.

Millie knew there was no way she would get back to sleep without knowing if there was some sort of threat coming Hunter's way. How awful it must be to be targeted by disgruntled people who didn't get their way in court proceedings. It didn't bear thinking about. She pushed back the covers and slipped on Hunter's shirt that he had left hanging over the back of a chair. It came to just above her knees but at least it offered a small measure of modesty. She padded downstairs to the sitting room, where Hunter was speaking to someone on his phone. His head was bent forward, he had a deep frown on his face and he was pinching the bridge of his nose.

'Okay, I'll be there as soon as I can.' He clicked off the phone and turned and saw her standing there. 'Sorry. I have to go out for a bit.' His expression became shuttered, like curtains being pulled down on a stage.

Millie frowned. 'What for? What's happened?'

'Nothing.' He began to move past her in quick strides.

She caught his arm on the way past. 'It can't be nothing if you have to go out in the middle of the night. Was it one of those calls?'

He looked at her blankly. 'What calls?' His tone was blunt to the point of rudeness.

'The threatening calls you told me about, just then upstairs.'

'No.' His eyes flicked away from hers. 'It's…something else.'

'What, though?'

A flash of anger backlit his tawny gaze. 'What part of "go back to sleep" are you having trouble understanding?'

Millie straightened her spine and met him glare for glare. 'What part of "I want to know what's going on" are you having trouble understanding?'

He held her feisty look for a pulsing moment. But then he expelled a heavy breath, the anger going out of him with a weary drop of his broad shoulders. 'Look—I don't mean to be rude, but this is something I'm best left to deal with alone.'

'I shared my body with you tonight, Hunter. That was a big deal for me. At least have the decency to share with me what's going on. How do I know you're not going out to a booty call or something?'

Hunter let out another ragged sigh. 'It's my sister. She's having a difficult moment. I have to go to her to help settle her down. Her carer is not coping.'

Millie rapid-blinked, her own anger at his intractability leaking out of her like air out of a punctured balloon. 'Her carer? Emma needs a carer?'

His expression was grim. 'Yes. Her favourite one is on leave at the moment and she's having trouble adjusting. I won't be long. Just go back to bed and I'll see you in the morning.' He turned to leave the room but Millie followed him.

'I'm coming with you.'

'No, Millie. Please. This is not your affair. It's mine.'

She wasn't taking no for an answer. How could she go back to sleep *in his bed* as if nothing was the matter? 'Hunter, I'm coming with you, even if I just sit in the car and wait for you. It's three in the morning. You might fall asleep at the wheel coming home and cause an accident.'

He was either too tired to stand up to her or something about her argument got through to the lawyer in him at last. 'Okay. But be quick. I haven't got time to waste.'

Millie was so quick getting dressed, she could have set a world record. She followed him out to the car, and they were soon on their way. It had rained during the night and the streetlights cast starbursts of glistening light on the road. It seemed to take for ever, but in reality it was only a short time later when Hunter pulled up in front of a lovely little townhouse nearby.

He opened his door and glanced at her, his features set in somewhat bitter lines of resignation. 'You'd better come in. I don't like the thought of you waiting out here alone in the car.'

'Okay.' Millie didn't give him time to come round and help her out—she was beside him on the footpath before he'd even got out himself.

Hunter used his own key to open the front door and led the way into the house. Millie got the sense that as soon as he crossed over the threshold he forgot she was even there— he was focussed intently on going straight to his sister. She hung back, caught between wanting to help but also not wanting to intrude. She could hear sobbing from one of the bedrooms and then the gentle soothing of Hunter's deep baritone.

'Hey, poppet, what's all this fuss about, hmm? Shh. I'm here now.'

There was the sound of sniffling. 'I had a bad dream that Rupinder decided not to come back. She's going to, isn't she? She promised me she would come back.'

'Of course she's coming back,' Hunter said. 'She's just looking after her mother for a bit. She'll be back in a couple of days.'

Millie couldn't stop herself from approaching the bedroom. She stood in the doorway and caught the eye of the carer who was standing to one side looking rather helpless. Hunter glanced over his shoulder as if he sensed Millie's presence. A mixture of emotions passed over his face in a lightning-fast moment—annoyance, frustration, despair. It was the despair that made her step further into the room, thus capturing Emma's attention.

'Hello,' Millie said with a smile. 'You're Emma?'

'Yes, who are you?'

Millie came closer to the bed. 'I'm Millie. I'm a…friend of your brother's.' A friend? A lover? It was hard to describe exactly what she was to him now. A fling partner?

Emma's gaze swung to Hunter, a smile lighting up her features. 'Are you going to marry her? She's very beautiful, like a princess.'

Millie could feel herself blushing to the roots of her hair, but Hunter took his sister's question with implacable calm. 'I don't think she would have me, poppet.' His voice contained a distinct note of ruefulness, but Millie knew it was for show. The last thing he wanted to do was marry anyone, much less her.

Emma glanced at Millie's left hand and frowned. 'But she's wearing an engagement ring.'

'It's not mine.' Hunter said.

Emma swung her gaze back to Millie. 'Whose is it?'

'My…erm…fiancé's. He passed away three years ago.'

Emma's brow wrinkled as she processed the information. 'Passed away?'

'He died,' Millie said, realising Emma might not understand the euphemistic term. 'He had a brain tumour.'

'My mummy died ten years ago,' Emma informed her gravely. 'But she's in heaven now, watching over me, isn't she, Hunter?'

Hunter gave a tender smile that sent an arrow straight to Millie's heart. 'Yes, poppet, she is. Now, it's time you got back to sleep and let Judy finish her shift. I need to get Millie home.'

So, he didn't intend to take her back to his place for what was left of the night. Millie fought back her disappointment, knowing it was completely understandable, given the circumstances. But she desperately wanted to talk to him about Emma's situation. It was clear the young woman had some sort of disorder, giving her an almost childlike understanding of the world. Why hadn't he told her about his sister in more detail? Or did he think that would have been a breach of Emma's privacy? All the same, Millie had shared so much of her own background, it didn't seem fair he hadn't trusted her with his.

Judy came out to the sitting room with them once Emma had settled back down with her princess nightlight on. 'I'm really sorry about tonight, Hunter. She got herself into a full-blown panic attack. I thought it best to call you.'

'You did the right thing,' Hunter said. 'She's still having trouble getting used to Rupinder being on leave. I'll clear my diary in the morning and take her out for brunch. I'll let the morning-shift carer know.'

They said their goodbyes and soon after Hunter led Millie back to his car. His expression was set in frowning lines and her heart ached for the burden he carried with regard to his sister. She waited until they were both seated in the car before she spoke.

'Hunter, I'm sorry if you thought I was intruding back there.'

He flicked her an unreadable glance as he tugged his seatbelt across his chest and clicked it into place. 'You *were* intruding. Emma doesn't cope with strangers all that well. You could have made a difficult situation so much worse.' His curt tone cut the air like a flick-knife.

Millie suppressed her desire to snipe back at him. 'I'm sorry. It must be so hard for you worrying about her all the time. You're an amazing big brother. She's so lucky to have you.'

He gripped the steering wheel even though he hadn't yet started the engine. His gaze was fixed straight ahead, his jaw locked tight, a pulse beating in his neck. 'Emma has a rare genetic disorder. So rare they haven't even got a name for it. She has complex medical issues that require twenty-four-seven care. So, forgive me for being a little over-protective.'

As apologies went, it certainly wasn't gold standard, and his tone was hardly what anyone could call friendly, but Millie didn't care about that. She cared that he had carried the burden of care for his sister for so long on his own. She placed her hand on his muscled thigh. 'You were being absolutely how you should be, given the stress you're under. I can't imagine how hard it must be to have the constant worry hanging over you. I thought my concerns over my mum were bad, but your situation with Emma is so heart-breaking.'

He released his grip on the steering wheel, his shoulders going down on a heavy sigh, his weary gaze meeting hers. He lifted a hand to her face and tucked a strand of hair back behind her ear, his mouth set in a rueful line. 'Thank you for being so nice to Emma. And so understanding.'

'I understand how hard it is to have someone you love limited by things outside of their control,' Millie said. 'My mother obviously isn't in the same category as Emma but it's certainly been a struggle at times.'

'You're a good daughter. I could see that the moment you came into my office that day. She's lucky to have you.'

There was a small silence.

Hunter let out a long breath, his eyes still on hers. 'I should get you home.'

Millie stroked her hand down his lean jaw, her gaze searching his. 'Is that what *you* want?'

His eyes lowered to her mouth and another serrated sigh escaped his lips. His hand went to the back of her head and inexorably drew her closer to his descending mouth. 'I think you know what I want.' His voice was a low, deep rumble that set her pulse racing and, before she could answer him, he covered her mouth with his.

His lips moved against hers almost angrily at first, as if the night's stress had found an outlet in blistering passion. But then his lips gradually softened into an exquisite tenderness that made her heart squeeze. He held her face in his hands and his tongue glided through her parted lips, playing with hers in a sexy tango that sent her heart rate soaring.

He finally eased back to look down at her, his hands still cradling her face. 'The night of our blind date? I'd come straight from the hospital. Emma had a *grand mal* seizure. She has milder ones occasionally but this one was serious.' His mouth twisted. 'That's why I wasn't in the best of moods.'

Millie threw her arms around him and hugged him tightly. 'Oh, I'm so sorry. And I was such a cow to you that night. What a shallow person you must have thought me. I'm so ashamed, now I know what you had to deal with. You must have been out of your head with worry.'

He put her from him to smile at her. 'Don't beat yourself up too much. It didn't stop me noticing other things about you.' His hooded gaze dipped to her mouth once more.

Millie brushed her finger over his bottom lip, her skin catching on the rich crop of stubble just below. 'It was the anniversary of Julian's passing… I always find that day hard, but not for the reason most people think. I don't even know why I agreed to go on the date with you, other than Beth and Dan kept at me to get out more. I guess I thought, if I went once and it was a complete and utter disaster, then they'd let it drop.'

Hunter stroked her cheeks with his thumbs in a slow caress, his eyes holding hers. 'Don't you think it's time to be honest with your friends about what you felt for Julian? Keeping up the pretence is hurting you, holding you back from living life to the full.'

Millie pulled away from his hold and sat back in her seat and fisted her hands in her lap. 'It's not just about me, Hunter. I have to consider Julian's mother.'

'Why?'

She flashed him an irritated glance. 'Why? Because he was her only child and she lost him. And if I tell her I didn't love him, and would never have promised to marry him if he hadn't got sick, what do you think that will do to her? It will destroy her.'

Hunter placed a hand on her shoulder, but she shrugged it off. 'Hey, aren't you second-guessing how his mother might react?'

Millie looked down at her tightly knotted hands, her engagement ring winking at her, as if to remind her of her impossible situation. 'I know Lena well. We've spent a lot of time together over the years. I've spent more time with her than my own mother. I don't want to do anything that will cause her further pain. Now, please, can we just get going? Judy will wonder why we're sitting out here for so long.'

Hunter started the car with a sigh, and put it into gear and eased out of the parking space. 'I think it's best if I run you home instead of coming back to mine. It's almost time to get up anyway.' There was nothing in his tone to suggest he was annoyed with her, but she sensed his frustration all the same.

'Fine.'

The evening hadn't gone as either of them had planned, and yet she understood far more about his situation now. It gave her an insight into his character, his love and concern for his sister more than obvious. His tenderness towards Emma had been so touching to witness. Millie could only imagine how his sister's health issues had impacted him over the years. And his mother's death, which must have been such a cruel blow on top of everything else.

There was a long silence broken only by the swishing of the car tyres on the rain-slicked roads.

Hunter pulled up outside Millie's flat in Islington and she turned to him. 'Thanks for dinner and…everything. And for letting me meet Emma. She's very sweet.'

Something flicked over his features like a zephyr rippling across sand. 'Yes, she is.' He turned off the engine and got out of the car, striding round to her side with an inscrutable expression on his face. The rain had slowed to a half-hearted drizzle and the sounds of the city waking up sounded in the distance—a far-off siren, the rumble of a delivery lorry, the distinctive sound of a London cab.

Millie stepped out and touched him on the forearm. 'I meant what I said earlier. You are an amazing brother to Emma.'

Some of the tension in his features relaxed and he gave a rueful half-smile and covered her hand with his. 'Sorry our first night together ended the way it did. Let's see if we can do it better tomorrow night, hmm?'

Millie licked her dry lips, her pulse already racing with anticipation. 'Don't you mean tonight?'

He gave a light laugh and pulled her up close. 'So I do.'

CHAPTER NINE

HUNTER DROVE BACK home wondering if he'd been a fool to allow Millie to come with him on his middle-of-the-night mission to calm his sister. He had always been so careful to keep his lovers away from Emma. They were temporary, and had no long-term place in his life, and therefore none in his sister's. But Millie's response to Emma and her immediate, intuitive and compassionate understanding of the situation touched him deeply.

How could it not? He'd been carrying the weight alone for so long that sharing it with someone, even for a moment, was heartening. She got it. So many people didn't. The stress of never being able to relax in case there was another crisis just around the corner. The sense of always being on duty, the background noise of persistent worry overshadowing every other thing in his life.

The night had been a show-stopper in so many ways. He'd always suspected making love with Millie would be wonderful, but he hadn't been prepared for just how wonderful. Her passionate response to him was electrifying and he couldn't wait to make love to her again. His body craved her like a forbidden drug, but he knew he would have to be careful not to get too addicted to her. He had his fling rules written in stone in his head and nothing and no one—not even someone as delightfully entertaining and gorgeous as Millie Donnelly-Clarke—was going to change them.

Her openness about the situation with her late fiancé had been humbling. He was not the heart-on-the-sleeve type, but he could still understand how difficult it must have been for her to reveal the depths of her anguish over her past relationship. He understood the way guilt could grind you down, eat away at you until you could taste it in your mouth and feel it swirling in your gut. The fact that Millie had let him into her private world of pain had in some ways made it easier for him to let her into his. Was that why he hadn't insisted on her staying in the car? Why he had taken her with him instead of dropping her at her home first? He could have put his foot down.

He smiled to himself when he thought of her feisty reaction to when he commanded her to do something. But he liked that about her, right? Her push-back was a turn-on. She stood up to him, challenged him and dared him to do differently, which in the long run could be a problem. A big problem. Even the most closed off part of his brain sensed the dangerous territory he was drifting into. He had allowed her closer than he had allowed anyone in years, possibly ever.

But, hot damn, it felt good, and he would enjoy it while it lasted.

When Millie came out for breakfast the next morning, Zoey was sitting at the kitchen table with a tub of yoghurt in front of her and a teaspoon halfway up to her mouth. She put the spoon down and her mouth shaped into a teasing smile. 'I'm surprised you're up at this hour, given how late you came in. Dare I ask where you were and what you were doing until almost daybreak?'

Millie checked the water level in the kettle and then switched it on. 'It was certainly a night to remember.' She took out a mug from the cupboard and turned to look at her friend.

'I met Hunter Addison's sister, who has a disability. She's lovely.'

'He took you to meet his sister? Oh, and here I was thinking you had bed-wrecking sex with him all night and—'

'I did. Well, before I met Emma, that is.'

Zoey's eyebrows shot up. 'You actually slept with him?' Her gaze went to Millie's left hand for the briefest of moments. 'Wow. I wondered if you'd ever get back on the horse, so to speak.'

Millie turned back to the hissing kettle and, placing a tea bag in her mug, poured the boiling water in. 'Yes, well, I was wondering about that myself.' She jiggled the tea bag a few times and then took it out and popped it in the bin beside the counter. She came back and sat at the table opposite Zoey, cradling the mug in her hands.

'So, how was it?' Zoey was leaning forward, her face alive with intrigue.

Millie could feel her cheeks growing as hot as the mug in her hands. 'It was amazing.'

'Are you seeing him again or was that just a one-off thing?'

Millie put the mug down on the table between them. 'We're having a fling, but I want to keep it quiet for the sake of Julian's mother.

It's only a fling. It's not going to go anywhere. But I don't want her to feel I'm cheapening Julian's memory by having it off with a notorious playboy.'

Zoey frowned. 'Do you really think Lena is going to mind if you finally move on with your life?'

Millie pushed a tiny crumb on the table a few millimetres away with her finger, her gaze lowered. 'She will find it difficult, of course. How could she not? If I were to one day marry someone else and have the children she thought I was going to have with her son, then how else do you think she'd feel?'

Zoey sat back in her chair with a thump. 'I think you're overthinking it, truly I do. She might be pleased for you. Yes, of course she will always be sad about losing Jules, but I don't think she would want you to lock yourself away for ever.'

'I can't risk it.'

Zoey made a snorting noise of disdain and leaned forward again, her violet gaze probing. 'But what you do *you* want? Do you want to spend the rest of your life wearing a dead man's ring, never knowing what it feels like to be a bride, a wife, a mother? All the things you wanted so badly with Jules?'

Millie placed her hands around the mug again and stared at the dark liquid inside. How long could she keep this dreadful pretence up? Especially with her friends? She had told Hunter. Maybe it was time to tell Zoey and Ivy too.

She slowly lifted her gaze back to Zoey's searching one. 'The thing is… I didn't want those things with Julian.'

The silence was so intense, the air seemed to ring with the echo of her words.

'You didn't?' Zoey's tone was beyond shocked, her mouth hanging open. 'But I thought—'

'I know what everyone thought,' Millie said, whooshing out a breath. 'And I encouraged them to think it. I wanted to end things with Julian even before he got sick. He didn't seem the same person to me, and he certainly wasn't once he'd had the first round of surgery. Thinking back now, it was probably the brain tumour growing that first changed him, and then the surgery made it worse.'

'Oh, Millie…' Zoey seemed completely lost for words, which was somewhat out of character for a girl with a razor-sharp intellect and rapid-fire tongue. She reached across the table and grasped Millie's hand. 'Why didn't you say something earlier?'

'I couldn't. I felt so guilty. How could I have told him it was over when he had just been diagnosed? Or just after surgery or when he was in and out of remission? It would have been cruel, not just to him but to his mother too.'

'And all this time you've carried this...' Zoey's eyes were suspiciously moist, and her throat rose and fell as if she was trying to gulp back a sob. She leaned back again and brushed at her eyes with an impatient hand and added, 'Gosh, now you've made me cry, and nothing *ever* makes me cry.'

Millie wondered if Zoey's self-confessed hard heart was quite as tough as she made out. Zoey was good at the tough-as-nails façade, just as Millie was good at being the heart-sore fiancée left all alone. Once you played a role long enough, it became an entrenched part of your persona, sort of like a typecast actor. 'I know, it kind of snowballed, you know? One decision turns into two decisions and then three and four and, before you know it, you're trapped in a web of your own making.'

'Would you have married him if he had lived a few more days?'

Millie lifted one shoulder in a shrug. 'I know this sounds weak and pathetic of me, but I probably would have. It's amazing what guilt will make you do.'

'I don't know why you should be feeling guilty. You didn't give him the cancer.'

'I know, but once he had it I gave him hope, and I couldn't bear to take it away from him when he needed it the most.'

Zoey pushed back her chair and came round and wrapped her arms around Millie's shoulders. Her friend wasn't normally a physically demonstrative person, so the hug meant a lot. 'Jules was lucky to have you by his side. You did what you thought was the best thing at the time but now you have to think about what you want.' She pulled back to look at Millie. 'And, if you want Hunter Addison, then go for it.'

'Even if it's only for a fling?'

Zoey shifted her mouth from side to side, deep in thought. 'Not ever having had a fling myself, I can't advise you on that. But, hey, if you're going to have one, maybe I will too.' She picked up her tub of yoghurt and the teaspoon. 'I just have to find someone as hot as Hunter Addison. Wish me luck?'

Millie smiled. 'Be careful what you wish for.' But she might as well have been saying it to herself.

The following day Hunter was relieved to hear that Rupinder was back on duty with Emma now that her mother was making a good recovery. After taking Emma out for brunch—and hearing her chatter incessantly about how nice Millie was, and asking when she could come for a visit again—he finally settled her back in at home. He was determined there would be no more visits from Millie. It wouldn't do to get Emma's hopes up when all he and Millie were doing was having a short-term fling.

A friendship between his sister and Millie was out of the question, even if a part of him acknowledged that Millie was exactly the sort of person who would be good for Emma. She was sweet, compassionate and understanding. She didn't gawk or stare or ask intrusive questions. She accepted Emma as she was and for that he was immensely grateful. But a cosy little friendship between his sister and Millie couldn't happen.

He handed Emma over to Rupinder with the confidence to know it would be unlikely he would be called in the middle of the night, for the time being. It gave him the freedom to slip away for the weekend with Millie—the next hurdle, of course, would be convincing Millie to come with him at such short notice.

He decided to call her at work between clients, wishing he had the time to go and see her in person. He knew he was acting like a hormone-mad schoolboy with a crush but he couldn't seem to help it. His mind was preoccupied with her, reliving every moment they spent together making love. His body was on fire for her, eager to experience again the mind-blowing passion they had created together. He was used to having good sex, he was a competent and sensitive lover, but he had never had such off-the-scale sex. Was it the novelty aspect? Millie wasn't exactly his standard fling partner. She hadn't even liked him the first time she'd met him but in a way that had added to the attraction. The challenge of winning her over had fired him up in a way he had never been before. But that fire would have to go out at some point, right?

He couldn't—*wouldn't*—allow their fling to morph into anything else.

* * *

Millie reached for the buzzing phone on her work desk. Her heart gave a skip when she saw Hunter's name pop up on the screen. 'Donnelly-Clarke Jewellery Design, Millie speaking.' She used her most professional tone in an attempt to keep a little distance. It wouldn't do to answer the phone to him in a breathlessly excited voice like a lovesick schoolgirl. She was a fully grown woman who was having a simple fling. Casual. No strings. How hard could it be?

'Hello, Millie speaking,' Hunter drawled.

She leaned back in her chair and tried not to notice the way her insides quivered at the sound of the deep, sexy burr of his voice. 'Hi. How was your brunch with Emma?'

'It was good. Rupinder is back, so Emma is happy.'

'Oh, that's nice,' Millie said. 'I'm so glad. You must be relieved.'

There was a small silence.

'Are you free this weekend?' Hunter asked.

Millie ran her tongue over her lips. 'Erm, I might be. What did you have in mind?'

'Champagne. No clothes. A plunge pool. Sex. On a private yacht in the Aegean Sea. Have I tempted you?'

'You had me at champagne.'

He laughed. 'What time can you be ready?'

'What time do you want me?'

'I want you now.'

Millie shivered from head to foot at the rough desperation in his tone. 'I want you too. Last night was…wonderful.'

'Apart from Emma interrupting things.' There was a rueful edge to his voice.

'I didn't mind. I enjoyed meeting her.'

'So, can you be free at six? I'll book flights. It'll be a late night, but worth it when we get there.'

'Sure.' Millie put down the phone a short time later, wondering why he had so swiftly changed the subject back to their travel arrangements when she'd said how much she had enjoyed meeting his sister. He hadn't even acknowledged her comment. Did that mean he didn't want her to visit Emma again? Was he somehow ashamed of his sister? But that didn't sit with her understanding of his love and care for Emma. He was devoted to her, going out of his way to make sure she was safe, secure and well looked-after.

Or was it because Millie was only a temporary phase in his life? She had no permanent footing and he didn't want Emma getting too attached to her. But surely Emma was entitled to have relationships independent of her brother?

Millie barely had time to get home from work and pack before Hunter's pick-up time. They got to the airport and checked in, and soon after boarded their flight. First class, of course. She sat back with a glass of champagne in her hand and smiled at him. 'Is this how you spend your free time? Flying off to Greece to sail off into the sunset?'

'I wish.' His mouth twisted. 'I haven't been on the yacht for months. I'll probably have to whack away the cobwebs as we board.'

She gave a tiny shudder. 'You're joking… right?'

He grinned at her, his whisky-brown eyes twinkling. 'I have staff who maintain the boat for me. I call them ahead of time and they prepare the food and so on.'

Millie toyed with the stem of her glass, her eyes following the movement of her fingers rather than hold his gaze. 'I guess you've done this a few times now? Taken a lover away for a sex-fest weekend?'

Hunter picked up a strand of her hair and curled it around his finger. 'I've taken groups of people—colleagues, friends, that sort of thing—but never a lover by herself.' There was a husky quality to his voice.

Millie turned her head to face him, wondering why she was the first woman he had chosen to spend the weekend alone with on his yacht. He was looking at her mouth with a hooded gaze, his fingers still playing with her hair, sending shivers dancing down her spine. 'Careful, Hunter. You're making me feel rather special.' She injected her tone with teasing playfulness. 'We're having a temporary fling. You don't have to make me fall in love with you.'

His hand fell away from her hair and every muscle on his face froze. 'It would be most inadvisable for you to do so.' His lawyerly tone was strangely jarring. Of course she wouldn't be so foolish. He didn't need to remind her of the terms of their liaison. She had drawn a line under falling in love with anyone ever again. She had once thought she loved Julian, but that had been a teenage love that all too soon had faded once tested. How could she be sure a future love for someone wouldn't do the same?

Millie gave another playful smile. 'Have

you considered the possibility *you* could fall in love with *me*?'

Something moved at the back of his gaze with camera-shutter speed. 'No.' His answer was brutally blunt, his gaze now screened.

Millie gave him an arch look. 'No, as in you've not considered it, or no, as in you don't think it's a possibility?'

He held her gaze with a steely determination. 'It's a possibility I will strenuously avoid giving any traction whatsoever. But while we're on the subject—I don't want my sister to develop feelings for you either.'

Millie frowned. 'So, what does that mean? You don't want me to visit her with you?'

'It would be best if you didn't. She has a tendency to form strong attachments to some people and, when those people leave, she's devastated. I've learned the hard way to keep things simple where she's concerned.'

'But don't you think she's entitled to have friendships of her own? She needs social contact beyond her carers, surely?'

'She has a handful of friends at a nearby group home she visits now and again.'

'But surely she needs more than that?'

Hunter's mouth tightened. 'You don't understand how difficult it is for her. She has the mentality of a small child. She believes what people say, and then they go and do the opposite, and it almost destroys her.'

'Like when your father left? Is that what happened?'

'Yes.' There was a bitter light in his eyes.

Millie placed her hand on his tense forearm. 'And you were the one who was left to pick up the pieces.' She spoke softly, desperate to show she had some understanding of picking up the pieces after someone had their heart broken. Hadn't she done it for her mother time and time again?

He glanced down at her hand on his arm before meeting her gaze, his hand coming over the top of hers, holding it in place. 'She cried for weeks. My mother and I tried to console her, but it was impossible. She used to sit in the front window of the flat we were living in, waiting for him. It was heart-breaking to watch. She would sit for hours like that.'

'Oh, how sad,' Millie said, blinking back the sting of tears. 'Why do you think your father deserted Emma and you? I mean, he was divorcing your mother, not you and Emma.'

Hunter took her hand and held it between each of his, one of his thumbs massaging the back of it in an almost absent fashion. 'He was one of those fathers that never failed to tell us he loved us. He spoilt us, buying us lots of expensive presents at birthdays and Christmas. We lived in a nice house in a well-to-do suburb. But, once Emma's condition became a little more obvious and lot more difficult to manage, he got cold feet. He didn't want a damaged child. He wanted a perfect family so everyone could pat him on the back and say, well done.'

'That's so selfish.'

'Tell me about it.' His tone was wry. He rolled his thumb over the diamond on her ring in the same absent fashion. 'It turned out he'd been having affairs for years on his business trips away. The presents were his guilt offering, I suspect.'

'You haven't seen him since?'

'No. He didn't even come to Mum's funeral. Didn't even send a card or flowers.'

Millie gripped his hand. 'I can only imagine how hurtful that must have been. I've never known what it's like to have a father— mine died before I was born. And none of my stepfathers were great stand-ins, in that sense. But to have one you truly believed loved you and then be rejected by him is just soul-destroying.'

He gave a movement of his lips that wasn't even close to a smile. 'Yes, well, I got over it pretty quickly, but Emma still asks about him occasionally. She has the deep-love gene. I don't.'

Or had he suppressed it in order to avoid further hurt? 'If he came back and asked for forgiveness, would you give it to him?'

'No. There are some things you can never forgive.' His gaze met hers again and he added, 'The words "I'm sorry" are like the words "I love you". So easy to say, but whether people mean them or not is another thing.'

Millie wondered if there would ever be a time when Hunter would say those words—*I love you*—to some lucky woman. Or had he become so jaded and embittered by the hurt his father had caused that he would never risk it?

She raised her champagne glass to his in a toast. 'Here's to never falling in love.'

Hunter tapped his glass against hers, his gaze unwavering. 'Here's to sticking to the rules.'

But Millie had a strange feeling those rules were just begging to be broken.

CHAPTER TEN

HUNTER HADN'T BEEN wrong about the late
night, Millie decided when they finally arrived in the wee hours of the morning to col-
lect his yacht, moored just outside of Athens.
Luckily she had dozed on the plane, so she
wasn't feeling quite as wrecked as she might
have been. Hunter led her on board in the
moonlight and she looked around in wonder
at the magnificently appointed ocean-go-
ing craft. It was like a floating hotel, with a
plunge pool on deck and a hot tub, and sun
loungers set up to make the most of the view
once at sea.

The streamlined elegance of the yacht only
added to the air of supreme and decadent lux-
ury. Inside was a deluxe kitchen and dining
area, and a lounge area off that leading to a
home theatre. The master bedroom was on
the level below and had a bank of wide win-

dows with a set of sliding doors that wrapped around two-thirds of the room, offering a spectacular view, even at night.

Millie knew she was giving a very good impression of a child let loose in a sweet shop, but she couldn't help it. She gazed around at everything, touching the butter-soft leather of the sofas and the velvet scatter cushions. 'Oh, my…it's just amazing, Hunter. How you ever tear yourself away to fly back home to work is a mystery to me. I'd want to stay here for ever.'

'I'm not sure what Emma would have to say about that if I never came home. Or my clients, for that matter.'

She turned from stroking her hand over a brass fitting on the wall to look at him. 'Have you brought her on board?'

'No. It's too complicated with her medical needs. She needs to be close to a hospital in case anything goes wrong.'

She came over to him and linked her arms around his neck, toyed with the ends of his dark hair above the collar of his shirt. 'The worry must eat away at you all the time. Can you ever relax?'

He smiled and drew her closer. 'Aren't I relaxed now?' His eyes glinted, his body hardening against hers.

'You feel quite tense to me,' Millie said with a smile. 'But maybe I could help you with that? How does that sound?'

'It sounds like heaven.' And his mouth came down and captured hers.

The sleepiness she had felt earlier completely disappeared, her body alive and wanting him with heated fervour. She opened to the thrust of his tongue, welcoming him into her mouth with a whimper of delight. His hands got working on her clothes and, as each piece was removed, her excitement grew. He pressed kisses to her neck, each of her breasts and down her sternum, kneeling in front of her to anoint her most intimate flesh with his tongue. She broke apart within seconds, shuddering under the magic of his touch, waves of ecstasy rippling through her entire body.

He straightened and, still holding her by the hips, drew her against him once more. 'See what you do to me? I'm crazy for you.'

Crazy enough to fall in love with me?

The thought popped into her head and she couldn't get it out. She didn't want him to fall in love with her...did she? She certainly didn't want to fall in love with him. They had agreed to keep their feelings out of this. To keep things casual. But what was casual about experiencing the most mind-blowing pleasure of your life with the man of your dreams? For Hunter was all that and more, she realised in that moment. He had qualities and values that aligned so well with hers. How could she stop herself from admiring him? How close was admiration to love? It was barely a footstep away and she had to be careful not to take it.

Millie slithered down his body and set to work on the zipper of his trousers. 'Let's see if I can make you a little crazier.'

He placed a hand over hers. 'You don't have to do that.'

She looked up at him. 'But I want to.'

'Are you sure?' His eyes glittered with anticipation, his body tense as a coiled spring.

Millie stroked her hand over his turgid length through the light barrier of his underwear. 'I wouldn't offer if I wasn't sure.'

Which was a new thing for her, she suddenly realised. With her fiancé, she had often done things she hadn't wanted to do just to please him. But with Hunter she wanted to please herself as well. Touching him in this most intimate way was almost as pleasurable as when he did it to her. It was a mutual expression of intense desire, and one thing she was sure of when it came to Hunter Addison—she had intense desire for him.

She finally got his underwear and trousers out of the way and leaned closer to stroke her tongue down his steely length in a cat-like lick. He shuddered and his hands grasped her by the head, his legs almost buckling as she went back for more. She licked and stroked him, suckled and drew on him, until he was quaking with the need to let go.

But he wouldn't let her go that far. He dragged her up to her feet, his eyes dark, glazed and wild with lust. 'I want to be inside you. Now.' His tone was ruthlessly determined and within seconds she was lying on her back on the king-sized bed, her breathing hectic as he quickly sourced a condom.

And then bliss…

His thrusts were hard and fast, as if he had finally allowed himself the freedom to express the explosive desire that rocketed through his body. Millie was with him all the way, relishing the almost primal way of coupling—the mutual desperation to get to the highest point of human pleasure.

She went over the edge first with a high cry,

her body shuddering as each crashing wave tossed and swirled and hurled her around in a tumultuous sea of sensation. Hunter followed with his own powerful release, his body finally sagging against hers in the aftermath, his breathing still heavy.

Millie ran her hands down the length of his strong back and shoulders, enjoying the muscled weight of him on top of her. Enjoying the quietude after such an earth-shattering experience. How had she not realised making love could be this amazing? She had been short-changed in her relationship with Julian, which was partly her own fault. She had settled for second best. Held on to a flagging relationship out of a sense of duty and despair rather than deep and abiding affection. The sort of affection that could withstand anything thrown at it, even illness, even terminal illness. She hadn't loved Julian like that. She had never loved him like that.

But she was worried she *could* love Hunter that way. Deeply worried.

Hunter eased himself up on one elbow to gaze into her eyes, one of his hands idly playing with a few strands of her hair, letting them slip through his fingers before capturing them again. 'I'd really like to stay here in bed with you like this, but I have to get this vessel out to sea.' He dropped a kiss to the end of her nose and added, 'I considered employing a skipper I use sometimes, but I didn't want anyone else on board in case I can't control myself around you.'

Millie stroked her finger down the length of his strong nose, a teasing smile lifting up the edges of her mouth. 'Don't tell me the notoriously iron-clad self-control of Mr Hunter Addison is getting a little shaky around the edges?'

His eyes darkened and his mouth came inexorably closer to hers. 'You'd better believe it.' And then his mouth swooped down and covered hers.

Millie woke to the dawn sunshine pouring in through the bank of full-length windows in the master suite. The streaks of pink and red with an indigo backdrop that were reflected in the ocean were beyond spectacular.

She left Hunter peacefully asleep beside her and got out of bed. She picked up the silk wrap she'd brought with her and slipped it on, loosely tied it around her waist and padded over to the window, staring out at the view in wonder.

It would be a photographer's dream to see such exquisite colour and light, the hues changing with each passing second, the intensity of the sun as it peeped its golden eye above the horizon promising a beautiful day ahead.

In the distance she could see a faint disturbance in the smoothness of the sea's surface, and then the distinctive shape of a dorsal fin, soon followed by the smooth silver back of a breaching dolphin. And then eight or more followed the first, and she gasped out loud as they breached in tandem, as if following some sort of ancient aquatic choreography. 'Oh, wow! Hunter, look—dolphins!'

The sheets rustled as Hunter threw them off and he came and joined her by the window, completely and utterly naked. He placed his arms around her waist, standing behind her, drawing her back against his body. Being so much taller than her, he had an uninterrupted view of the ocean and its pod of playful dolphins over her right shoulder. And she had the delight of feeling his hardened body pressing against her bottom.

'Nature at its finest,' he said, and began to nibble her right ear.

Millie shivered and turned in his arms,

winding her arms around his neck, but not before a greedy glance at his morning erection. She gave him a sultry smile. 'That's for sure.'

He lowered his mouth to hers in a long, drugging kiss that made her forget all about the glorious sunrise and sea life. His proud length throbbed against her belly, a potent reminder of the pleasure she had experienced in his arms in the early hours.

'Where are we?' she asked against his lips.

'In heaven.' He nudged her lower lip with his mouth. 'Or at least, we soon will be.'

Millie laughed and kissed him back. 'I meant apart from sensual heaven. I must have fallen asleep after you got the boat moving last night.'

'I've taken us far enough away for us to have some privacy. A mate of mine has a private island a short distance from here. We can moor there, so we can have a picnic on the beach.'

'That sounds amazing. I think I'm going to remember this weekend for the rest of my life.'

He smiled a lazy smile. 'Never let it be said I don't know how to show a lady a good time.'

'You're definitely excellent at doing that.'

Hunter brought his mouth back to hers in a scorching kiss that made every hair on her head rise in a Mexican wave. Her blood began to pound in her core, swelling her most intimate tissues, making them throb with a delicate pulsing ache that only he could assuage. His tongue danced with hers in an erotic imitation of love-making and she all but melted into a pool of longing.

He broke the kiss to peel the silk wrap from her body and it slipped to the floor at their feet. His hands ran down from the tops of her shoulders to her hips and back again—slow, caressing, mesmerising strokes that made her pulse race with anticipation. His gaze was sheened with lust, glittering, primal lust of a man who wanted a woman so badly it was killing him to stay in control. It thrilled her to think she was able to stir him up so much, and only fair, given the sensual havoc he caused her. Her body trembled under his touch, aching with need, hungry to feel the hot, hard friction of his body within hers.

'Make love to me. Please.' She didn't care that she sounded as if she was begging. Damn it, she *was* begging.

'Don't you want breakfast first?' There was a teasing glint in his gaze.

'Later.' She bit gently on his lower lip and added, 'I'm hungry for you right now.'

Hunter lifted her as if she weighed nothing more than a feather pillow and laid her on the bed. He came down beside her, his hands stroking her body into a frenzy of want. He circled her belly button with a lazy finger, tiptoeing it lower, lower, lower until he got to her feminine folds. Her back lifted off the bed in heady anticipation, her breath catching in her throat. He separated her and gently began to caress her already sensitive flesh, his eyes watching her response as if spellbound.

Millie was the one who was spellbound. Spellbound, mesmerised, dazed by the sensations he was creating in her body. Spasms, contractions and flickers of pleasure darted through her flesh, tension building, the ache for release increasing in intensity. She was getting closer and closer to the edge, the build-up tightening every nerve to a centre of concentration. And then she flew up into outer space, the sensations ricocheting through her body with rocket-ship speed. Spinning her round and round until she was gasping with the sheer bliss of a planet-dislodging orgasm.

Hunter waited until she was coming back

to earth before he applied a condom and moved over her, turning her so she was straddling him, his hands holding her by the hips. His eyes were dark and lustrous with desire, his erection full and thick inside her. She squeezed herself around him, rocking with him, watching the contorted expression of pleasure play out on his face. It excited her to see him as undone by her as she was by him just moments ago. His pace increased, her pace increased, his groans and gasps matching hers. And then they were both riding the wave together, spilling out the other end in a tangle of limbs, the sound of their ragged breathing the only sound other than the sea lapping at the hull of the boat.

Millie lay across him, her head buried in his neck, breathing in the scent of him, storing it in her memory for the time when she would no longer be with him. How long would it be? A week or two? A month? A couple of months? He hadn't specified the time frame, only that their fling would be temporary.

It occurred to her that one day in the not-too-distant future he would be photographed by the press with someone else. Someone who would occupy his bed for a short time and be completely satisfied with the arrangement.

The thing was, could *she* truly be satisfied with a fling?

You're going to have to be. Those are the rules.

Millie rolled over onto her back and untangled her legs from his, her thoughts still in turmoil. Was she making another prison for herself? Her prison with Julian had been the lack of true love. But her prison with Hunter would be an over-supply of it.

If she fell in love. If. Such a small word for a massive change of circumstances. Circumstances Hunter was at pains to avoid, no matter what. And so had she been, until now…

Commitment. Life-long love. Marriage and children.

Those were the things she had denied herself, pretending she didn't want them any more. But the truth was, she hadn't wanted them with Julian.

Hunter reached for her and gathered her close, rolling onto his side, resting on one elbow. He brushed hair away from her face with his other hand, his mouth tilted in a wistful smile. 'This was a great idea, stealing you away for a weekend.' He interlaced his fingers with hers. 'I wish I could keep you with me longer.' His voice went down a semitone, low and deep with a trace of huskiness.

Longer as in past the weekend, or longer as in for ever? The unspoken words seemed to hover in the silence. Millie returned his smile and lowered her gaze, circling each of his hard, flat male nipples with a slow-moving finger. 'We both have our businesses to run. A long weekend is about the only holiday I get these days.'

'Are you breaking even? Making a profit?'

Millie gave a slight grimace. 'I was until I had to help Mum out.' She sighed and added, 'That's why it means so much to me that you waived your fees. It's the most generous thing anyone has ever done for me.'

He leaned forward and pressed a soft kiss to her mouth, pulling back to look at her with a hooded gaze. 'My career has never been about making heaps of money. I enjoy the financial reward, and I've had good results with investments and shares and so on, but it's not something that drives me.'

He gave a rueful twist of his mouth and continued, 'I wish there had been someone who could have helped my mother during the divorce. It still sits like a stone in my gut that she got so done over. She believed everything my father told her. He spun her lie after lie after lie. I know it killed her in the end—the stress of him leaving her practically destitute and with a disabled child to take care of. It tortures me that she might have survived her blood cancer if she'd been stronger, both physically and mentally. But she just seemed to get ground down and then stopped fighting.'

He took a deep breath and let it out in a ragged stream. 'It was the saddest day of my life when she passed away.'

'Oh, Hunter,' Millie said, reaching up to stroke his face with a tender hand, tears clogging the back of her throat. 'I'm sure she would be so proud of how you take care of Emma. And how you've set out to help other people with your work. You truly are the most wonderful man. I'm even more ashamed now that I didn't see it the first time I met you.'

One side of his mouth lifted in a smile and he brushed his thumb over her lower lip, sending tingles through her flesh. 'You're making me sound like a saint, and I'm hardly that.'

Millie stroked his jaw, delighting in the sexy rasp of his stubble against her fingers. 'I've been thinking about Emma and how she's so reliant on you when Rupinder is away. Have you thought of getting her a therapy dog?'

Hunter frowned. 'A dog? Are you crazy? She can't take care of herself, let alone a dog.' His tone was dismissive, and a coldness came over his face that chilled her to the bone. He moved away from her and scooped up a pair of undershorts and stepped into them. 'Look—sorry to be blunt, but Emma is my problem, not yours.'

Millie sat up and pulled the sheet up to cover her body, suddenly feeling naked and exposed under his searing gaze. 'Have I upset you? I didn't mean to. I was just offering a suggestion that—'

'That is unwelcome, unworkable and un- necessary.' He turned his back on her to con- tinue dressing, his movements jerky with barely suppressed anger.

Millie pushed away the covers, got off the bed and slipped on the bathrobe, tying the waist ties with equally jerky movements. 'I don't understand why a simple suggestion should trigger such a response in you. I was only trying to help.'

Hunter turned to face her, his expression dark and forbidding. 'I've been responsible for my sister for years. I know what works and what doesn't, and a dog would make things way more complicated than they already are. Dogs need to be walked and fed, and trained appropriately. Emma isn't capable of it.' He blew out a breath and added in a weighty tone, 'And dogs rarely outlive their owners. What would that do to Emma if the wretched thing dies?'

Millie bit her lip, understanding his logic, but also seeing the other side of the argument. 'No pet comes with a guarantee of a long, healthy life, but a therapy dog is trained to be a companion and helper to people with disabilities. They come fully trained for the person's needs. Perhaps you could ask the carers to help with the walking and feeding? And maybe Emma is capable of more than you give her credit for. She could groom it, at the very least. The dog would be with Emma all the time, night and day. It would provide continuity and comfort when Rupinder or whoever goes on leave. Dogs can be sensitive to mood and can be trained to detect when a seizure is about to happen. Surely there are more positives than negatives in getting one?'

His expression became one of grave reflection, as if he was mentally sorting through her arguments in a logical and sequential fashion. Then, after a long moment, he finger-combed his hair and let out another long, serrated breath. 'Look—I'll think about it, but I'm not making any promises.'

Millie smiled and approached him, placing her arms around his waist and looking up into his eyes. 'I seriously don't think you'll be disappointed. You've had a dog before—I saw the photo at your house. It looked like you were great mates.'

A shadow flickered through his gaze and he gathered her closer. 'I had a dog called Midge but she had to be given away when we moved into a tiny flat after my parents' divorce. That was the second-saddest day of my life.'

Millie tightened her arms around him, as if reaching back in time to comfort the young boy who had lost his faithful friend in such a heart-wrenching way. 'That's terrible, Hunter. So terribly sad. How did Emma cope with that?'

'She didn't.' Another deep, ragged sigh. 'In the end, I had to pretend it was no big deal to me so I didn't ramp up her distress.'

Millie leaned back to gaze into his shadowed eyes. 'I can see now why you got so triggered by my suggestion of a therapy dog…'

He gave a glimmer of a smile, his arms a strong, warm band around her. 'You have a habit of triggering me in lots of ways.'

'Good or bad triggers?'

He bent down to press a light-as-air kiss to her lips. 'I think you already know the answer to that.' And his mouth came down and covered hers in a spine-tingling kiss.

CHAPTER ELEVEN

AN HOUR OR SO later, Hunter anchored the yacht a short distance from the private island and, using the Jet Ski that was housed in a special section of the craft, took Millie and a picnic breakfast to the secluded cove. She hopped off the Jet Ski into the shallow water and waded the rest of the way to the golden sand.

If she had been asked to imagine paradise, then this would have been it. The beach was accessible only by boat or Jet Ski, and vertiginous cliffs rose on either side of it, creating absolute privacy. The beach was about four hundred metres in width and the water the quintessential deep Aegean blue, and as you got closer to the shore, the more shallow water, with its sandy bottom, became a stunning turquoise and then a gorgeous cyan.

'This is just...amazing...' Millie could

barely find the words to describe the exquisite beauty surrounding her.

'It is pretty special.' Hunter leaned down to put the picnic hamper and their towels on the sand. He straightened and smiled. 'Breakfast or swim first?'

Millie laughed and began to strip off her shorts and top, leaving just her bikini on. 'Definitely a swim.'

His eyes roved over her from head to foot, his pupils darkening with unbridled lust. 'You don't need your bikini.'

'Are you sure?'

His gaze smouldered. 'Absolutely.'

Millie untied the strings of her bikini top and tossed it to the towel he had laid down and spread out just moments before. Next, she untied the strings at her hips, letting the bottoms fall to her feet. Never in her wildest dreams had she ever thought to be standing naked in front of a gorgeous man on a jaw-droppingly beautiful beach. Nor had she ever thought said man would look at her as if she was even more stunning than their surroundings.

'Aren't you going to get undressed?' she asked.

'Sorry. I got distracted by the view.' He

hauled his white T-shirt over his head and tossed it to the towel. Next came his shorts and underwear and Millie couldn't drag her eyes away from his gloriously male body.

Hunter held out a hand to her and she slipped hers into it, shivering at the scorching look in his brown eyes. 'Have you ever skinny-dipped before?'

'No. I seem to do lots of things with you that I've never done before.' *Like fall in love.*

Millie knew she had taken the fatal last footstep and was now madly, fiercely, desperately in love with him. How could she not be? It had been stupid of her to think she could keep her feelings out of their arrangement. Their arrangement was all about feelings. Feelings she had never felt before. Feelings that had sparked at their first meeting, flickered into a bright flame at their second and by their third she'd been all in. Engulfed by desire, which she had fooled herself was only a physical thing. A mutually driven lust that would burn out in time.

But it wasn't burning out, it was burning brighter, hotter, more intensely.

And, like a silly little moth, she was flying right into the heart of the blistering flame.

* * *

Hunter led Millie into the warm water, determined to refrain from making love to her until after they had a swim. But it was hard. Damn hard. She looked like a beautiful mermaid, slim with curves in all the right places, her hair a long silk curtain down her back. But making love in the water was tricky when it came to condoms and the one thing he wouldn't do was make love without a condom. The last thing he needed was another complication in his life, and an unexpected pregnancy would top the list.

He held her hand until they were waist-deep and then turned her into him, running his hands down the sides of her body, his own body thick, tight and hot with desire. 'We're supposed to be swimming,' he said, leaning down to nibble at her ear lobe, breathing in the scent of her until he was almost drunk with it.

'I'm not stopping you.' She nestled closer, sliding one of her hands down between their bodies to stroke him.

He pulled her hand away even though it almost killed him. 'Yes, you are, little minx.' He tapped her on the end of the nose and added, 'Hold that thought until after breakfast.' He gave her bottom a playful pat. 'Now, go and swim.'

Millie gave him a mock pout and then turned and swam off with neat fluid strokes. He watched her, spellbound for a few seconds, before striking out after her. She was a lot harder to catch than he'd expected, and he had to up his kick-and stroke-rate to get to her.

He finally caught her around the waist and trod water with her, smiling down at her sparkling eyes and laughing mouth. 'Now I've got you.'

Her legs wound around his waist and her naked body tempted his to the point of pain. 'So you have. But not for long.' Water droplets clung to the end of her long eyelashes and her lips curved upwards in a smile that made something in his chest tighten like a vice.

Not for long... The words were a jarring reminder of the time frame on their fling. *His* timeframe. But that was the way he wanted it, wasn't it? He couldn't offer her anything other than this—a short-term fling that would burn out just like any other had in the past.

So why, then, wasn't it burning out?

There was no boredom on his part, no sense of claustrophobia or dissatisfaction. The sex was mind-blowing, her company and conversation were stimulating and he enjoyed every minute he spent with her. Yes, even when she offered unwelcome suggestions about getting a therapy dog for Emma. Millie had made him think about it, more deeply than she probably realised.

And she had got yet another secret about his childhood out of him. A painful episode that had left its mark on him to this day. Saying goodbye to Midge was the hardest thing he had ever done. Letting his beloved pet go had ripped his heart out. He had taught himself at that moment never to love anyone or anything so much that he was unable to say goodbye. He had always known he would one day lose his parents, as most children expected to do. And he had always known he would one day lose Emma because her condition precluded a long life.

And he would say goodbye to Millie at some point and be fine with it, just as he had been fine with it with everyone else.

Hunter brought his mouth down to hers in a blistering kiss that sent his blood hammering through his veins. Lust swept through him and he grasped her by the hips and held her against his pounding length, relishing the silky feel of her body so temptingly close to his. His tongue played with hers in a cat-and-mouse caper than sent his heart-rate up and his self-control teetering. He wanted, wanted, wanted to sink into her velvet wetness and take them both to paradise. He wanted, wanted, wanted her with a driving, drumming ache that was beyond anything he had ever felt before.

He set her down before him and lowered his mouth to her breasts, her nipples already tightly puckered. He tasted the salt water dotting her flesh, and the scent of her fresh-summer-flowers fragrance sent his senses haywire. He caressed her other breast with his lips and tongue, enjoying the sounds of her pleasure. Enjoying the sensual power he had over her. But, hey, didn't she have the same power over him? So much power it was driving him crazy, turning him into a man of such desperate need, it raised a red flag in his head.

How long would this continue? This driving need for her that wouldn't abate. It had to peter out eventually. It *had* to. Otherwise he was in deep water.

'I want you so badly it's becoming a problem.' He didn't realise he had spoken his thoughts out loud until Millie caressed his jaw with her soft little hand, her eyes shimmering with need.

'Why is that a problem?'

Hunter stroked his hands down from the top of her shoulders to grasp her by the wrists. 'I can't make love to you without a condom.'

'You brought some with you, though, didn't you?'

He nodded towards their towels and hamper. 'They're back with the towels.'

She tiptoed her fingers down his sternum to his belly button, hovering tantalisingly close to his jutting erection but without actually making contact. His blood thundered and roared, and he had never felt so turned on in his life. Her eyes were dancing, her lips curved upward in a smile that was as sultry as the sunshine beating down on his head and shoulders.

'Then maybe we'd better get back to the towels before you or I lose control.' Her voice had a breathless edge and there was a gleam of mischief in her eyes.

Hunter had a feeling he was the one in far more danger of losing control. Her hand drifted lower, her fingers going around him, and he let out a curse through tight lips. 'Your touch drives me to distraction.'

'That's only fair, since yours does the same to me.' She squeezed him tighter, an on-off squeeze that sent his pulse racing.

Hunter moved her hand away and scooped her up in his arms, walking back through the waist-deep water to the sandy beach. 'I think that's enough swimming for now.'

Millie laughed and linked her arms around his neck. 'Spoilsport.'

He laid her down on the towels and quickly rummaged for a condom and applied it. He came over her, pinning her with his body, wanting her so badly he had to count backward to slow himself down. He drank in the sight of her shining eyes and slightly parted mouth, her rosy-red lips eager for his kiss. Her legs opened for him and he surged into her wet warmth with an agonised groan of pleasure, his skin peppering in goose-bumps as her inner muscles wrapped around him. He set a fast pace, but she was with him every step of the way, urging him on with gasps and groans and whimpers that thrilled him to the core of his being. She wanted him and he wanted her and that was enough for now.

It had to be.

* * *

Later that day, Millie and Hunter sat on the yacht after showering and changing and shared a glass of wine as the sun went down. Every inch of her body felt alive and tingling, and every time she caught Hunter's eye a frisson would pass over her flesh as she recalled their explosive love-making on the beach.

But then one of the thoughts she was fighting so hard to suppress crept up on her and began to taunt her. Would he one day bring someone else out here and make mad, passionate love to her? Would he wine and dine them and make them feel like a princess for the weekend? No doubt there would be numerous women after her—he was a playboy, after all. A man who wanted no ties, no long-term commitment.

Millie traced her finger round the rim of her wine glass in a reflective manner. 'You know, you've set rather a high benchmark for any other lover I might have in the future.'

There was a silence broken only by the gentle lap of water against the hull of the yacht.

Millie chanced a glance at him to find him wearing a brooding frown, his fingers tightening around his wine glass. He appeared to give himself a mental shake and his frown disappeared from his forehead, but not his eyes. It lingered there in the background like a shadow.

'So, you think you'll be ready to move on with your life after…us?' The slight hesitation over the word 'us' could have meant nothing or everything, but how could she tell? His tone gave nothing away.

Would she be able to move on? If he was coming with her on the journey then, sure, it would be a cinch. But without Hunter by her side, the man she had fallen in love with so deeply… How would it be possible to move on without his love in return? Millie stretched out her legs and crossed her ankles, twirling her top foot this way and that. Her left hand was resting on her thigh. The lowering sun caught the top of her engagement ring and she pointedly looked away, not wanting to be reminded of the mistakes she had made in the past.

'I'm not sure…' She gave him a forced little smile and added in a lighter tone, 'So, who will be the next woman you bring out here to impress?'

His frown deepened and he put his glass down on the table between them on the deck. 'I didn't bring you out here to impress you,

Millie.' His voice was low and had a deep note of gravity.

'Why did you bring me, then?'

His eyes held hers in a tight little lock that seemed to go on for endless seconds. She counted every one of them with the hammering beats of her heart. Boom. Boom. Boom.

'I brought you here because I wanted to be alone with you.' His tone dropped half a semitone to a deep burr.

'We were alone at your house in London.'

His mouth twisted. 'Until Emma needed me.'

Millie twirled the contents of her glass, looking down at the whirlpool she'd created, so similar to her swirling thoughts. 'Is Emma one of the reasons you don't want to settle down and have children of your own?' She raised her gaze back to his. 'Because you're worried you might have a child with a genetic disorder like hers?'

Hunter leaned forward to rest his forearms on his bent thighs, his broad hands flat against each other in the space between his knees. He let out a long breath, his expression hard to see at that angle, but she suspected he hadn't lost the frown.

'I saw what Emma's condition did to my

parents. As soon as it became obvious Emma couldn't be cured, my father bolted. My mother never lost hope that one day Emma would be miraculously healed. It was painful to see her scrabbling the money together for numerous alternative-health therapies. She went without to get Emma yet another experimental cure. None, of course, worked. Emma is a child locked in an adult's body. Nothing is going to change that. She will never get married and have children. She will never enjoy the things most people take for granted. I just try and make her life as comfortable and happy and secure as I can.'

Millie moved closer so she could touch him on the forearm. 'I think what you do for Emma is wonderful. Which makes me think you'd make the most wonderful father yourself. It seems a shame to rule out the possibility. You couldn't possibly turn out like your father. It's not in your nature. And think of the joy you'd bring to Emma if she became an auntie. She would love her nieces and nephews to bits, I'm sure.'

Hunter straightened but something about his tight expression cautioned her that she'd stepped over a line. 'Careful, Millie, it sounds like you're dropping hints about making our fling into something it's not.' His tone had a chilled edge that made her spine stiffen.

Millie removed her hand from his arm as if it had been burned. 'I wasn't doing any such thing. I was simply suggesting—'

He stood so abruptly, she flinched. 'You're very good at suggesting but not so good at understanding the implications of those suggestions.' The derisive edge to his voice cut her to the quick, the flash of his brown eyes even more so. He turned his back and gripped the ledge on the side of the yacht, staring out at the dipping sun, and added, 'Let's not ruin a perfectly nice weekend arguing over things that aren't important.'

Millie rose from the seat and came over to him but didn't touch him. She stood beside him, glancing up at his brooding expression. 'What could be more important than your happiness?'

He turned his head to look down at her, his top lip curled. '*My* happiness? Don't you mean your happiness? That's what this conversation is all about, isn't it?'

'I'm not sure what you're suggesting but...'

He pushed himself away from the side of the yacht, sending a jerky hand through the thickness of his hair. 'You're suggesting we make our fling permanent. That I pop a ring on your finger and marry you and have a bunch of babies. That just about sums it up, doesn't it?' His biting tone and cold gaze lashed at her nerves, already on edge.

Millie opened and closed her mouth, not sure how to respond. Those were exactly the things she wanted him to do, but not out of duty or because of her expectations, but because he loved her and wanted to be with her for the rest of his life. What a time to realise how much she loved him—the same time he was bluntly making it clear he didn't love her back.

'I would never want to tie anyone to me, as I once tied myself to my fiancé, out of a sense of duty or expectation. I would only want someone to be with me because they loved me too much to be away from me.'

Hunter glanced at the ring on her left hand, his expression still set in tight lines. 'Then maybe it's time you took that ring off.'

'Maybe it is.'

'But don't expect me to put one in its place because that is not going to happen.' His words were delivered in an adamant tone, his gaze glittering with disdain.

Millie raised her chin, determined not to

show him how crushed she was feeling. 'I never expected you to. You say you don't want the things other people want, just like I used to do. You're punishing yourself, denying yourself the most basic joys that life can offer, because you feel guilty about Emma. You are not to blame for her genetic disorder. You are not to blame for your father abandoning your family. You are not to blame for your mother's death. But you are to blame for not opening your heart to the possibility of love.'

Hunter stood with his hands low on his hips. 'Nice little speech, sweetheart.' His tone was cuttingly scathing. 'Let me guess what made you fancy yourself in love with me. Was it the house in London? The yacht? My private island?'

His island? Millie frowned in confusion. 'It's not your island. You said it belonged to a friend.'

He gave a grating laugh. 'Yes, well, that didn't seem to work with you, did it? You apparently saw through my little white lie and decided a man who owned a private Greek island was worth falling for.'

Millie's spine was so stiff, she swore she could feel every muscle bunching into knots. 'Are you calling me a gold-digger?'

'I'm calling you a romantic fool who got a little in over her head.' His expression was so cold, she wanted to shiver. 'I should have known this could never work. You're not the fling type. You were with the same man until he died, and you still wear his blasted ring.'

Millie automatically twisted the ring on her finger, testing to see if she could get it off, but it was still stuck. 'I explained my reasons for staying with Julian. I told you more than I've told anyone. I opened up to you, but you told me so little about yourself. I found out about Emma only by circumstance. I suspect if we hadn't been together that night at your home in London I would *still* know nothing about her.

'You're a closed book. You don't allow anyone close because you don't like giving people the power to hurt you. But life isn't truly a life if we lock ourselves away from the possibility of hurt. Life is all about hurting, and dealing with and healing those hurts the best way we can, surrounded by those we love and trust to help us through the best and worst patches. That is what I want in a future relationship—knowing someone has my back in the same way I have theirs.'

Hunter was still frowning darkly, his mouth

tightly compressed, a muscle beating in jaw. 'So, the question is, what do we do now?'

Millie knew exactly what she had to do but doing it was going to be the real kicker. But she had dawdled too long in the past and got trapped in a prison of her own making. She would not allow herself to do so again. She had learned her lesson and learned it well. Too well, for this time it really hurt. It hurt in a way she had never thought possible. Her heart physically ached inside her chest—ached like it was being compressed in a vice. 'Hunter, we have to end this. I have to end it. I can't see you again, or at least not in this context. Of course, I'll still attend meetings with my mother, unless you'd rather not—'

'Don't be ridiculous,' Hunter cut in. 'I will continue to act for your mother regardless of what's gone on between us. I can organise a support person for her if you'd rather not be there.' There was nothing in his tone to suggest any engagement of his feelings. He spoke clearly, politely, dispassionately, unemotionally. His expression also showed no sign of any disappointment, and his earlier anger had completely disappeared. It was as if he had stepped into another persona, a business-as-usual persona that had not been one bit affected by her decision to end their fling.

Millie searched his features for a long moment, clinging to the hope that there might be a tiny chink in his armour, but in the end she had to accept the inevitable. It was over. They were over. And she hadn't even told him she loved him, nor would she. He wouldn't want to hear it anyway. 'Thank you for…everything. I had a great time.'

His lips moved in a vestige of a smile, but it didn't reach his eyes. 'Glad to hear it.' He let out a short breath and swung away. 'I'd better get this yacht back to its moorings. We have a flight to catch in the morning.'

'Hunter?'

He glanced over his shoulder, his hand still on the railing. 'I'll sleep in the spare room tonight.'

She bit down on her lip, a little surprised and somewhat embarrassed he had read her mind. 'Fine. Thanks. I think that's best.'

On the painfully long journey back to London Hunter was determined that he would not reveal how disappointed he was with Millie's decision to end things between them. It was always going to happen, right? It just stung

a little that she had ended it before he had.
He was the one who usually walked away—
that was something he had perfected over the
years. Knowing when enough was enough,
knowing how to read the signs that things
were getting a little too serious. He was a
master at avoiding messy break-ups. And he
wasn't going to sink to the level of grovel-
ling now, even if he could eke out a few more
weeks of their fling. And it would only be a
matter of weeks—he didn't ever let a relationship go much longer than that.

But somehow the short time with Millie had made him hungry for more. Raven-
ously hungry. Awakened a need in him he
hadn't known he possessed. A need for a
deeper connection with someone, a mutually satisfying relationship where the usual
guards were down and inner vulnerability
exposed. She hadn't told him straight out that
she loved him, but he could read between
the lines enough to know she wanted more.
Much more. But he wasn't the person to give
it to her, so the wisest and surprisingly hardest thing to do was let her go. Surprising, because walking away from a fling had never
hurt in the past. It had never sat uncomfort-

ably with him, annoyed him or agitated him in any way whatsoever.

But boarding the plane back to London, sitting beside her and acting with indifferent politeness, was one of the most excruciating experiences of his life.

They walked off the plane together but, when they got to the exit, Millie turned to him with a look of resignation on her face. 'If you don't mind, I'll make my own way home from here.'

'Don't be silly, I'll drive you.'

Her small, neat chin came up and her eyes glinted with determination, and something in his chest collapsed like a sail. 'No, I don't think that's a good idea.' She held out her hand. 'Goodbye, Hunter.'

He ignored her hand, not trusting himself not to haul her back into his arms and remind her of all the reasons they should continue their fling a little longer. Why was this hurting so much? It was crazy. He never allowed anyone to get under his skin. Never.

He stripped his face of all emotion, determined not to show his inner turmoil. Determined not even to acknowledge it to himself. Why should he care they were over? It was a fling, damn it. Flings were meant to end sooner or later. 'Goodbye, Millie. I guess I'll see you in court.'

'Let's hope it doesn't come to that.' Her stiff little smile didn't quite reach her eyes, but it reached his heart like a sharp little dart.

Then she turned on her heel, walked out through the exit and he stood watching her go without moving a muscle to go after her. But then, why would he? He wasn't in love with her. He wasn't a believer in the romantic fantasy of happy-ever-after. He was a realist, a cynic, a man who knew how to avoid messy emotional entanglements.

And, by letting Millie go, he knew in his bones he had avoided one of the most potentially messy of them all.

CHAPTER TWELVE

MILLIE GOT HOME to her flat to find Zoey on her way out to visit her father.

'How did your weekend go?' Zoey asked, shrugging herself into a lightweight jacket and lifting her dark hair out of the collar.

'I'd rather not talk about it, actually.' Millie plonked her overnight bag on the floor with a despondent sigh.

Zoey frowned and walked over to her. 'It's over?'

Millie nodded. 'I ended it.'

'Why?'

Millie sank to the sofa and laid her head back against the cushioning. 'I don't want to make a fool of myself over him. I got out before I started gushing about how much I love him.'

Zoey's neat eyebrows lifted, her eyes wide as violet orbs. 'You *love* him?'

Millie pressed her lips together. 'Yes, well, it kind of happened before I could stop it.'

'Yeah, apparently it sometimes works that way.' Zoey sat down beside her. 'I'm sorry. How did he take it?'

Millie gave a gurgle of humourless laughter. 'Without a flicker of emotion. It kind of proves I did the right thing in ending it. If he cared a jot for me, you'd think he'd at least have said something, wouldn't you?'

Zoey shrugged one slim shoulder. 'I'm no expert on men, as you already well know. I have enough trouble understanding my own father without trying to understand men of our generation. But I do know one thing— you have to do what's right for you.'

'If it's right for me to end things with him, then why does it hurt so much?'

Zoey made an 'I'm sad for you' face. 'It really sucks to get your heart kicked around. But at least he wasn't unfaithful. And you ended it before it got really messy.'

Millie got off the sofa and began to pace the room. 'I need to do something to take my mind off this or I'll go crazy.'

'Come to dinner with Dad and I. You'll have a ball watching him get blackout-drunk and telling everyone in the restaurant how much he wished he'd had a son instead of a daughter.'

Now it was Millie's turn to do the sad face. 'I really don't know how you cope with him.'

'Yes, well, he's all I've got, so I have to suck it up.' Zoey got up and scooped her tote bag off the floor where she'd left it earlier. She hung it over her shoulder and added, 'I'm sorry it didn't work out the way you wanted it to. And if I wasn't such a cynic I'd say, hang in there. He might come to his senses and realise what he's given up.'

Millie's shoulders slumped on another sigh. 'I can't see that happening any time soon.' She dared not hope for such an outcome. It was in the realms of impossibility, knowing him the way she did.

Later that day, Millie unlocked the door to her studio and went to her workroom. She picked up one of her jewellery saws and passed it from one hand to the other, preparing herself for the thing she should have done long ago. A clean break was the best break. She began to saw through the gold band on her left hand, tiny sawing movements that finally released her from a promise she should never have made in the first place. 'I'm sorry, Jules.

I hope you're at peace now. I'm going to give this to your mum. I hope you don't mind.' She carefully placed the cut ring into an envelope and sealed the top down, placing it in her tote bag to deliver to Lena.

Millie sat down at her desk and began some preliminary sketches of a charm bracelet for Hunter's sister. She didn't want to walk out of Emma's life without leaving something behind to tell her she would be thinking of her. Hunter might not approve but she was determined to do it anyway.

Hunter threw himself into work in order to distract himself from thoughts of Millie. As usual, plenty of work was coming through the door—kind of proving his view of romantic love being nothing but a fantasy. He spent extra time and effort on Millie's mother's divorce, but he was still waiting on further details from Matteo Vitale over some missing funds and some suspicious offshore accounts. Matteo suspected a serious case of fraud and didn't want to act until he had all the facts on the table, but it held up the process, and meant Hunter couldn't get the closure he wanted.

He needed the distance.

He needed to stop thinking about Millie, period, but acting for her mother meant Millie was almost constantly on his mind. He was too much of a professional to let his bitterness over their break-up interfere with how he processed Eleanora's divorce. And he was still perfectly happy to do the work pro bono. It gave him a good feeling, and what he needed right now was good feelings because he felt rubbish most of the time. He had no appetite for food, no interest in the punishing exercise routine he usually enjoyed and no ability to hold a sensible conversation with anyone without his mind going elsewhere— most particularly to his island in Greece and the image of Millie walking out of the sea like a goddess.

Hunter groaned and snatched up his car keys and phone from his desk. Why couldn't he let it go? He was acting demented, like some sort of love-sick fool who didn't know how to walk away from a fling. He knew exactly how to walk away. He'd been doing it for most of his adult life. Why was it killing him now?

Because you miss her.

The words dropped into his head like stones in a pond, the circles going outward in waves with follow-up thoughts.

You miss her smile. You miss her touch. You miss her intelligence. You miss the lovemaking. You miss every damn thing about her.

So? He could go on missing her. He had no business picturing a happy-ever-after with Millie Donnelly-Clarke. There was no such thing as happy ever after, or at least not for people like him. He had Emma to think of— poor little Emma who would never be a bride, never hold her own baby in her arms. But he would do what he could to make up for that, using Millie's suggestion. Yes, he had listened and taken on board the notion of a therapy dog. He had one lined up that very day.

Hunter had arranged to meet the dog trainer and handler at Emma's townhouse. He hadn't told Emma anything about it, wanting to surprise her, as well as gauge her reaction in case she didn't warm to the dog at all.

He shouldn't have worried on that score, for as soon as the handler, Kate, brought in Ruby, the chocolate-coloured labradoodle, Emma wrapped her arms around the dog's neck and cried for joy.

'Do you really mean it? She's mine? All mine, to stay with me all the time?' Emma asked, happy tears shining in her eyes and dripping down her face.

Hunter smiled, in spite of his own misery, and felt a suspicion of moisture in his own eyes. 'Yes, poppet. Ruby is yours.'

'I can't believe it,' Emma said, petting the dog lovingly. Ruby lapped it up with a doggy smile and melting brown eyes and a wagging plume of a tail. A bond was forming right before Hunter's eyes and it touched him deeply.

But then he caught sight of a bracelet on Emma's wrist. 'Hey, poppet, where did you get that bracelet? Did Rupinder give it to you?'

Emma shook her head. 'No. Millie came by the other day. She made it for me. Isn't it beautiful?' She held out her wrist and swung the little charms around, making them tinkle. 'She's so clever. She told me to hold this charm here if ever I feel scared and lonely. See, this one? It's got a smiley face. I love it. But I might not have to hold it now I've got Ruby, huh?' She wrapped her arms back around the dog and Ruby's tail swept the floor like a shaggy broom.

Hunter suddenly felt tight in the throat and chest. Millie had taken the time to make Emma a bracelet. She had delivered it to

Emma and encouraged her to self-soothe, giving her a strategy with which to do so. Millie hadn't dumped his sister along with him. She had thought of Emma and taken it upon herself to make sure Emma was protected from any hurt resulting from their break-up.

What a pity Millie hadn't spared him the hurt in the first place. Maybe he needed a charm bracelet to rub every time he thought of her. He knew one thing for sure—he would have rubbed the metal to the thinness of paper in no time at all, so incessant was his thinking about her. He had a bad case of something, and he didn't want to admit it. The L word was hovering at the back of his brain, but he pushed it away. Love and hurt went hand in hand and he wasn't signing up for that any time soon.

But, oh, how dreadful it was to know he might never see Millie again. He would never hold her in his arms and kiss her or make passionate love to her. There was that wretched L word again. Sex used to be sex, but with Millie it was *always* making love.

Why had he been such a fool to let things go that far? Far enough to make him feel as if the bottom had dropped out of his world?

He had always determined never to love

enough to feel the pain of losing, yet he had lost Millie. But had he ever had her other than in a physical sense? From the outset, he had closed off his heart, only giving her his body. How could that ever be enough for someone as caring and loving as Millie? She wanted the whole package because anything less would be an insult. He was insulting himself, let alone her, not to open his heart to her.

There was a strange feeling in his chest, a loosening of bolts around the cage in which his heart was locked. It was like allowing a beam of light into a darkened, closed-off room, light that showed all the secret longings hidden inside. He had ignored and denied those longings for most of his life. Like his sister, he had been desperately hurt by their father, and had sworn never to allow anyone close enough to hurt him again. But he was hurting himself by not loving fully, openly and wholeheartedly. He was living half a life—he wanted more. Needed more. He needed Millie. She had challenged him from the start, triggering something in him which was only becoming obvious now.

Hunter leaned down to stroke the dog's silky ears and was rewarded with a lavish lick.

'So, you'll keep her?' Kate asked from a short distance away.

'Yes, I'll keep her.' Hunter had never been more certain of anything in his life, but he wasn't talking about the dog. Why had it taken this long to realise it? He was madly in love with Millie. Madly, deeply in love, and he had been a fool not to recognise it earlier. No wonder he'd been fighting it from the first moment they'd met. No wonder he was so miserable and lost. He was lost without the hope she gave him, the love she taught him to feel. She had unlocked his frozen heart, released him from his emotional prison.

He. Loved. Her.

'She's not yours,' Emma said, possessively hugging the dog to her chest with a fierce little stare at her brother. 'She's mine.'

Hunter laughed and ruffled Emma's hair. 'I'm not talking about Ruby, poppet.' He turned to Kate. 'Will you excuse me? Rupinder will fill me in with any instructions later. I have to propose to the love of my life.'

'Sure,' Kate said with a beaming smile.

'You're going to marry Millie?' Emma asked, eyes wide, smile wider.

'If she'll have me,' Hunter said. He leaned down and kissed his sister on the top of the head. 'Look after Ruby. She's part of our family now.'

And he hoped Millie was going to be too.

Millie walked back to her flat after visiting Julian's mother. It had been a poignant meeting, with tears on both sides, but it had given Millie some much-needed closure to hand Lena the engagement ring. She had soldered it together and put it back in its original ring box.

She hadn't told Lena she hadn't ever loved her son in a romantic sense. She didn't think it necessary, and nor did she want to taint the treasured memories Lena had. Instead, she'd told Lena she was now ready to move on with her life and hoped that Lena would find some joy of her own in spite of her loss. And, much to Millie's surprise, Lena announced she was actually seeing someone—her first relationship since Julian's father had left all those years ago. Her new beau was a widower with three school-aged children and Lena was already enjoying helping to take care of them.

Millie crossed the street at her usual place, lost in her thoughts—mostly of Hunter and how much she missed him—when she happened to look up and see him standing at her door. For a moment she wondered if her mind was playing tricks on her. She blinked a couple of times to reset her vision, but he was still standing there. She climbed the steps with unsteady legs, her heart racing. Why was he here? What possible reason could he have for coming here after they had said all that needed to be said?

'Millie, can I have a word with you?'

'Sure.' Millie was surprised at how even her voice sounded, given how fast her heart was beating. She began to work the key in the lock, but her fingers wouldn't cooperate. 'Sorry about this, the lock is a bit—'

'Here, let me.' His large hand came over the top of hers and turned the key with her, and the lock turned as smoothly as anything.

Millie removed her hand from under his and stepped inside, trying to ignore the tingling on her skin where he had touched her. Would she never be immune to his touch? He closed the door behind him and stood looking at her for a moment.

'You, erm, wanted to talk to me about something?' she prompted in a cool tone.

He let out a shaky breath, his hands seeming restless by his sides, his fingers opening and closing as if he was trying to control the urge to touch her again. 'I got Emma a therapy dog.'

'Oh, that's lovely. What's its name?'

'Ruby. Emma adores her already.'

'I'm so glad.'

A silence fell between them. A silence so thick, Millie heard herself swallow and suspected he did too.

'So, can I get you a drink or…?'

He stepped forward and grasped her by the upper arms, his expression tortured. 'My darling girl, can you forgive me for being a blind fool and not realising how much I love you?'

Millie stared at him speechlessly for a moment. 'You…you love me?'

His hands tightened on her arms as if he was frightened she was going to pull away. 'Madly. Deeply. Desperately. I think I fell in love with you that day we met for a drink, when you asked me to act for your mother. I've resisted it all this time, not even recognising what I felt as love until today. I've been flat-out miserable without you. I can't believe I let you walk away. I was so blind to what I was really feeling. Losing you made me finally realise how I was short-changing myself in life. My life can't be what it's supposed to be without you in it. I can't imagine life without you by my side. Please come back to me and make me the happiest man alive.'

She wrapped her arms around his waist and hugged him. 'I didn't want to walk away. I love you so much. I can't believe how much.'

He looked down at her with love shining in his eyes. 'Will you marry me? Please? Nothing would give me more joy than to have you as my wife and partner in life.'

Millie smiled and hugged him again. 'Yes, yes, of course I will, you darling man. How could you think I would ever say no to you? That was my problem almost from the moment we met. I saw what a danger you were to my heart. I tried to keep my feelings under guard, but it was impossible to resist you.'

He framed her face in his hands, looking down at her with loving tenderness. 'I'm a package deal, you know. It won't always be easy with Emma. Her health is tricky to manage, and she can be quite possessive over people. She's already glued to that dog.'

'I adore Emma,' Millie said. 'I hope you didn't mind that I visited her?'

He smiled. 'I saw the gorgeous bracelet. She loves it, and I can't thank you enough for not walking away from her because of me.'

'Do you think she could be one of our bridesmaids? I would love that so much.'

Hunter blinked back tears. 'You truly are a one-in-a-million girl. What have I done to be so lucky to have you in my life?'

Millie stroked his face with her hand. 'I'm the lucky one. I never thought it was possible to love someone the way I love you. I love you with all my being.'

'Do you remember when I told you how the pretence over your situation with Julian was hurting you more than anyone else? What a hypocrite I was. I realised I was doing the same. Hurting myself by not acknowledging what I really felt for you.'

Millie had never thought she would hear such wonderful proclamations of love from him. All her dreams were coming true. Her heart had never felt so full, her love for him knowing no bounds. 'I just love hearing you say how much you love me. I don't think I'll ever tire of hearing it.'

'I'm going to keep saying it for the rest of our lives.' He pressed a lingering kiss to her lips, then continued, 'I got to thinking about what you said about having children. Emma can't be a mother, but she would certainly love being an auntie. I want a bit of time with you first, since we've rushed our relationship so far, but let's have a family together.'

Millie pressed another kiss to his mouth. 'I would love to have a baby or two with you. Nothing would please me more. I didn't realise how much I wanted to be a mother until I met you. You will be the most wonderful father. I just know it.'

'And you will be a beautiful mother.' He captured her left hand and stroked his thumb over the vacant space on her ring finger. 'You cut it off.'

'Yes, I was finally ready. I gave it to Lena. She might end up using it herself, as she's seeing a nice man who has a young family.'

Hunter smiled and leaned down to kiss her. 'I can't wait to tell Beth and Dan about us. They saw the potential for us before we even met. That's kind of spooky in a way.'

'Spooky but lovely,' Millie said, kissing him back.

'Now, about a ring.' His tone was mock-business-like.

'Well, I could design one for you, if you think you can afford me.'

He grinned. 'I was hoping you would say that. I want no expense spared. I only want the best for my beautiful bride. I love you, my darling.'

Millie linked her arms around his neck and smiled against his mouth. 'And I love you right back.'

* * * * *

Blown away by
Breaking the Playboy's Rules?
Check out the first instalment in the
Wanted: A Billionaire trilogy
One Night on the Virgin's Terms

Also, why not try these other
Melanie Milburne stories?

One Night on the Virgin's Terms
His Innocent's Passionate Awakening
The Return of Her Billionaire Husband
Billionaire's Wife on Paper

Available now!